What people are sa

And this shall be my dancing day

In times all too quick to judge us and divide us, this patiently perceptive novel sees a deeper and more decent process: how the seeds of concern take root in ordinary, very different lives, sometimes in spite of ourselves; how our individual griefs and struggles can begin, by small unnoticed harms around us, to the possibilities in each other and ourselves... Not least, it suggests that the courage to take risks can open the door to new life.
Philip Gross, Winner of the T. S. Eliot Prize, 2009

In one phrase – I love it! She writes very well. It is so natural. It is like I am watching the scenes unfold instead of reading them off a page. Her writing is reminiscent of Margaret Drabble's novels.
Rebecca Riddell, Bookseller at Blackwell's Bookshop

A librarian living her narrow, orderly life recognises she has never lived. A civil servant struggles to reconcile her conscience with the populism of her political masters. Against a background of Brexit, migration politics and the horrors of trafficking, two women look for the strength to change and the courage to act, and in the process forge an unlikely sisterhood in a warm and moving parable about finding ways to grow into the light.

An easy, natural and involving read.
Paul Wilson, Portico Prize-winning author of *Do White Whales Sing at the Edge of the World?* and *The Visiting Angel*

And this shall be my dancing day is a small but perfectly formed joy to read! From the outset you are pulled into a mystery and are led to keep turning the pages to discover how things may unfold. As a former librarian myself Emma's character immediately intrigued me, a professional of the old school and I have met many like her. We follow her as she navigates life, her touching relationship with her neighbour Bob and her complex family dynamics, something we can all relate to. By modern standards she may be judged to have a "limited" life but far from it. As we go with Emma through the arc of the story Jennifer Kavanagh leads us to an optimistic and satisfying resolution.

Paul Joerrett, presenter of Bookylicious podcast and former university librarian

As soon as I got started on your book I sped through it, carried along at first by the details of Emma's limited life and narrow horizons, her warm relationship with Bob and the contrast with her confident, charismatic sister. And just when I thought I had the measure of the book, as a kind of study of loneliness, the plot suddenly turned on a sixpence into something darker and more alarming and I had to know how the characters' stories linked together and played out. I very much believed in Emma's emotional frigidity and her distaste for modernity, and I was glad that she was allowed to thaw at last. Many congratulations on a subtle and moving novel; I hope it does really well for you.

Clare Chambers, author of Women's-prize-longlisted *Small Pleasures*

And this shall be my dancing day

A Novel

And this shall be my dancing day

A Novel

Jennifer Kavanagh

ROUNDFIRE
BOOKS

Winchester, UK
Washington, USA

JOHN HUNT PUBLISHING

First published by Roundfire Books, 2023
Roundfire Books is an imprint of John Hunt Publishing Ltd., No. 3 East St., Alresford,
Hampshire SO24 9EE, UK
office@jhpbooks.com
www.johnhuntpublishing.com
www.roundfire-books.com

For distributor details and how to order please visit the 'Ordering' section on our website.

Text copyright: Jennifer Kavanagh 2022

ISBN: 978 1 80341 245 0
978 1 80341 246 7 (ebook)
Library of Congress Control Number: 2022908740

All rights reserved. Except for brief quotations in critical articles or reviews, no part of this book
may be reproduced in any manner without prior written permission from the publishers.

The rights of Jennifer Kavanagh as author have been asserted in accordance with the Copyright,
Designs and Patents Act 1988.

A CIP catalogue record for this book is available from the British Library.

Design: Stuart Davies

UK: Printed and bound by CPI Group (UK) Ltd, Croydon, CR0 4YY
Printed in North America by CPI GPS partners

We operate a distinctive and ethical publishing philosophy in
all areas of our business, from our global network of authors to
production and worldwide distribution.

By the same author
The Methuen Book of Animal Tales (ed.) 9780416247602
The Methuen Book of Humorous Stories (ed.) 9780416506105
Call of the Bell Bird 9780852453650
The World Is our Cloister 9781846940491
New Light (ed.) 9781846941436
Journey Home (formerly The O of Home) 9781780991511
Simplicity Made Easy 9781846945434
Small Change, Big Deal 9781780993133
The Failure of Success 9789781780998
A Little Book of Unknowing 9781782798088
Heart of Oneness 9781785356858
Practical Mystics 9781789042795
Let Me Take You by the Hand 9781408713143

Fiction
The Emancipation of B 9781782798
The Silence Diaries 9781789041828

Acknowledgements

Thanks are due to the following people, who generously shared their expertise. Any errors are my own.

Scott Albrecht, Cynthia Barlow, Jessica Bombasaro-Brady, Sarah Dodgson, Keith Hebden, Ben Jarman, Paul Jeorett, Jonathan Lingham, Jenny Moy, Kate Ulrick, Livi Webster, Crispian Wilson.

The phone call came in the middle of the night. I rolled out of bed and, to avoid disturbing Ian, took it in the other room. It's an image that has always stayed with me: that night when I stood naked in a dark room as I received the news of my brother's death.

Phil was four years younger than me, and had always remained my baby brother.

He had been such an adorable little boy. So solemn. With wide blue eyes when he asked sometimes the most uncomfortable questions, a habit that never left him. He cared about justice, responding to news of an atrocity or natural disaster with: "But why, Mummy?" Not surprising, really, that he went into the charitable sector. "Only the good..." And he did. Die young. It was unbearable.

Emma

Chapter 1

She would never have seen it if there hadn't been a bus strike.

For many years Emma had followed the same routine: every morning riding her old sit-up-and-beg down to the station, where she chained it up on the bike stands, before taking the train. At Victoria she usually took the bus. Until recently this had been her habit for winter only. In the summer she used to take her bike on the train and cycle at both ends of her journey, but since Southern no longer allowed bikes on rush hour trains she either took the bus or, on fine days, hired a bike from the stand near the station. Neither was ideal. Although the 507 was convenient enough, it was a bit of a hike at the other end, from Lambeth Palace to the club. And those stodgy low-geared bikes just weren't the same as her own. But her gentle ride to the station in the morning and back at night was good daily exercise – a wind up and a wind down, a transition from home to work and back.

So, because of the strike, Emma was on her bike on this chilly September evening. There was no telling how many times her bus had sailed along the main road, oblivious to what it was passing but, as it was, taking her usual shortcut down the little street on her way home, it stared her in the face. A bouquet of wilting flowers tied to the doorknob with a red ribbon like a bouquet left to honour the dead. The door was open, revealing a roughly carpeted flight of stairs which led straight and steeply into darkness.

Actually, as she braked to look more closely, she saw that it was not a bouquet, but a bunch of hand-picked flowers. Without protection, the flowers had drooped and wilted, were almost dry. With surprise she noticed among the lilies and roses a few stems of ranunculus, their multi-layered, tissue frilliness drained of life and colour, and only just recognisable as the flowers she had recently admired in her sister's garden.

The combination of gaping hole and wilting flowers made a surreal picture and, as she travelled home on the train, she wondered if she'd imagined it. But the image would not leave her and, now she'd seen it once, there was no ignoring it. Though she tried not to look too closely as she cycled to the station on the following nights, the flowers were always there. She didn't know why, but they haunted her. By the following Monday they had dried out even more. They were always there, and the door was always open. Why?

As if in answer, a month or so later on a glorious autumn day when she was once again on her bike, the door was shut. Or rather, with her attention on avoiding a pothole in the road, she rode past for once without noticing anything and only when she was sitting on the train home did she realise that she hadn't seen it; there had been no dark hole to attract her attention. She must have passed the door like any other.

On the way into work the next morning she deliberately took that route, although it meant dismounting to avoid going the wrong way down a one-way street. Instead of a dark interior she found a discoloured beige door – number 37, it was – and, to the right of it, hanging loosely from a grab rail, forlorn and disregarded, a bunch of flowers.

Wheeling her bike along the pavement, Emma came close enough to see a month-old notice in the downstairs window for a concert at St John's. Otherwise, the windows were blank and empty. Neither of the neighbouring houses showed any greater sign of life. To one side, a boarded-up window, and, to the other, grubby mottled curtains pulled across. If the houses were inhabited, there was no indication.

How Dickensian it all was! Maybe the door was open only at specific times. Maybe it was an office. No, with that sense of abandonment it was hardly likely. This sordid little place was either empty or had some more sinister significance. In either case, it was none of her business.

* * *

Emma lived near Leatherhead in Barleigh Common, a little row of semi-detached cottages, two up, two down. It no longer had a common and you couldn't call it a village: it was a hamlet which had been left stranded by the advent of a major road. The village shop had closed seven years before, and there was no pub or church within easy reach – not that Emma would have gone into either, but they might have provided focal points for their little community. As it was, apart from Bob next door, most of the residents were like her: commuters who spent little time in the area. But Emma loved her little piece of the country: the peace and quiet, her long narrow garden with fields beyond and, from her bedroom at the front, a view of trees.

Emma still found it strange to live south of the river. When she was a child, they'd always lived to the north of London, and when she'd moved into the city to study at UCL, she'd lived in Camden. The south had always seemed like a distant land. She'd had to get used to it, but was glad now that her arrival point was Victoria, north of the river, from where she had to cross back over the river to get to work. There was something psychological about crossing the river: a marker in the journey from home to work and back again. How bleak life would be without these transitions.

Today, as every day, Emma followed the wave of other sheep out of the station into the building chaos of Victoria. At Westminster Cathedral, she ducked out of Victoria Street into the welcome breathing space of the patio, and on to the bicycle docking station in a little road nearby. She released a bike and made her habitual way south.

As usual, she made the most of small road alternatives, zigzagging her way towards the river, but there was no avoiding

Lambeth Bridge, where roadworks rendered the pavement and cycle lane out of bounds. Even with the optimistic warning to motorists about the narrowing of the route, advising them "to avoid overtaking cyclists", it didn't feel any too safe, and there had been that awful accident during rush hour not so long ago, when a cyclist had been mown down by a lorry. But as Emma looked downriver, Westminster Bridge, with its cars, lorries, buses and the flashing light of a police car, didn't seem any less congested. Although Emma liked the ride along Queens Walk ("for considerate cyclists"), from one bridge to the other, she usually stuck with her normal route.

How she loved the river! *Earth has not anything to show more fair* – wrong bridge and not her favourite anyway, but never mind. She would still often dismount just to lean over the side and watch the boats chugging up and down – both the cruise boats and a few carrying some sort of freight. Some people apparently even travelled by boat to work. It was such a busy thoroughfare: it seemed entirely proper that the river should be used like this. A work-a-day mode of transport for an ancient and vibrant city.

Emma came to properly only as she arrived at the entrance to the club, where she blinked and smiled at the commissionaire, as he lifted his hat.

"Good morning, Joseph."

"Good morning, Madam. You keeping well?"

"Yes, thank you. You too, I hope."

The same words every day: for nearly thirty years they had provided a soothing start to her working day.

"Honestly, Em," she could hear her sister say, "it's positively feudal."

Maybe so, but also a bastion of civilisation. There was a benevolence, an old-world charm and good will that countered the uncaring hurly-burly of the journey in.

The modest entrance opened out into a hall of light and

spaciousness. The ground floor held only a public sitting room to the left and the members' dining room to the right. She never tired of the gracious sweep of the stairs up to the members' room on the first floor, and to her library – her other home. Whenever she asked herself why she subjected herself to the costly ghastliness of rush-hour travel, only to arrive at a polluted metropolis, she reminded herself that it was a means to an end, the end being where she was now.

All in all, there was a pleasing pattern to Emma's days, a routine that ironed away any fluxes that arose, and held at bay any deeper concerns. Returning home in the evenings, she would open the gate, lock her bike in the outhouse, and stroll up the garden path, tucking a wayward tendril from the wisteria round the drainpipe before letting herself in. Firstly, as she opened the door, acknowledging the enthusiastic welcome of her cats, then, with the two of them weaving round her ankles, making a tour of her little estate, noting the appearance of a new shoot since last she looked, picking off dead leaves or idly dead-heading a rose. Strange how something so simple should give such satisfaction. Freeing the plant to flower again; liberating its fertility. She now couldn't pass a plant without tending to its needs, and kept a watering can outside the back door for the demandingly thirsty pots. "Plants just have two needs," the gardener, Vince, had told her: "sunshine and water".

Slipping out of her work shoes, pouring herself a glass of wine, and feeding the urgently appealing cats – feeding time at the zoo – before making something for herself. "Come on, then. Anyone would think you hadn't eaten for weeks." Pinky and Perky were sisters, equable enough, and accustomed to what they did now, padding together across the vinyl floor to eat at adjacent plates. After supper, there would be TV or radio with a game of patience or sudoku, drawing the curtains as it got dark, feeling herself ensconced in the safety of her habitual life.

Emma was used to being alone. Since her mother died, she

had lived by herself and, apart from one brief blissful interlude, there had been no one special in her life. On the whole, her life suited her. Even if solitude had never been her choice, she was content enough. When she gave it any thought, she realised that she enjoyed the freedom, and doubted whether she would ever stretch her routines to make room for anyone else. It was a good life. Or, at any rate, it was her life, and she was used to it.

But that evening was different. Although she followed her usual pattern, Emma was distracted by the vision of a door open to a dark nothingness, a bunch of dying flowers tied with red ribbon. As she went through the usual motions, she felt accompanied.

Chapter 2

Emma had never been much of a looker. A skinny little thing, with glasses from an early age who'd allowed *men never make passes at girls who wear glasses* to enter into her sense of self. And it was no good telling her to try contact lenses: she had tried when she was about fourteen, and just couldn't stand the feel of something in her eyes. And now that she had a tendency to dry eyes, lenses were all the more impossible. It was the same with ear-phones – she just didn't like the intrusion of foreign bodies.

Growing up had been uneventful: Emma had been dutiful and studious; her mother kind if undemonstrative; and she and her sister got on well enough. The only time Emma had resisted her mother's wishes was on the matter of attending Saturday morning ballet classes. Mother wasn't keen on such a *physical* activity. For Emma, it was secretly a disappointment. Despite fantasies of graceful elegance conjured up by the graceful elegance of Fonteyn and Nureyev seen on a school friend's TV, she'd found ballet classes an effortful rather than a joyful experience. Nonetheless, she did quite well, and she'd persevered, not least because it was her only rebellion.

Emma had had few romantic expectations and anyway what she knew of "it" was all so mysterious and, well, embarrassing. She saw couples who seemed comfortable together, but there was nothing to say how they'd got to that point. She simply didn't understand how one got from here to there. But she was too shy to ask, and she didn't dwell on her perplexity: she was too busy with her studies, which gave her a quiet and meticulous contentment. As she grew up, she gradually came to terms with her looks and who she was. She was bright. Literary, from the word go. Language, books, writing: they were for her a deep abiding pleasure.

"Why classics?" Mum had asked. Indeed, that was more

perplexing. It had been hard to explain how she felt drawn to the treasures of a long-gone world. She mumbled something about languages that were the foundation of the English language. Greek wasn't taught at her school, but with Latin she would have a head start with any of the Romance languages. But that wasn't really it. She was drawn to the order and clarity of Latin: it was consistent; it made sense.

It was only later, at university, when she was introduced to the glories of Greek, that she realised that the attraction of classics was much more than an enabling of linguistic facility. She loved the flowing femininity of the language, and the way its structures exercised her mind. More than that, it was the whole world of antiquity that drew her, a world of symmetry and beauty. Maybe it was its distance that lent it a romantic gloss, like a longing for something once, or never to be, known.

Despite the fact that Nietzsche had said that no one could know what Greeks and Romans were, and therefore could not know whether he was suited for finding out about them, Emma felt that she did know, that she felt it in her bones: not so much the Romans, perhaps, who satisfied her need for order but were a bit on the heavy side. It was the Greeks in whose lightness and logic she felt a commonality: an order and symmetry open to the power of the unseen. The romance of the classical world: it was a strange paradox.

For her thesis, she had chosen the subject of *stasima*, the choral dances of Greek Tragedy, such an important aspect of their culture, and so hard for any modern reader to imagine. Without any experience of a stage presence, how could the layman grasp the true importance of these plays and how key the dances were to the continuity of the drama, their singing and dancing allowing the actors to change mask and costume between episodes without any illusion-destroying interruption.

Emma chose choral dance ostensibly because it was an under-developed subject for research. It was only some years later that she realised that the choice might have had more significance. As for her as a child, dance represented independence: it was an expression of the freedom (if only for men in those days) that so appealed to her about the Greek culture.

Emma might have gone the academic route if she hadn't come down with flu at the time of her finals and ended up with a 2.2. Despite her initial disappointment, Emma realised that perhaps it was just as well. She couldn't imagine standing in front of a roomful of students and speechifying. It was the research that interested her, and she could continue with that anyway. Her tutor suggested librarianship as something suitable for her interests and her academic turn of mind. So she applied to the library school at UCL and got in. She would have preferred to have gone further afield, but UCL had the best course, and living at home would be cheaper.

During the last months of her librarianship training, Emma kept an eye out for possible openings. Although her determination to stay within the field of classics helped to focus her search, it also severely limited the possibilities. The Institute for Classical Studies was fully staffed; the Athenaeum too had a well-established librarian, and was in any case too generalist for her tastes. So it was with wonder and gratitude that she happened upon an ad in *The Times* for a librarian at the Antworthy club.

From then on, her days were peopled with men. It wasn't until she began working at the club that she saw how very male the world of classics was, and wondered if its attraction for her had something to do with having been brought up in an all-female household. It was certainly odd, working in such a male establishment and, as the club had never allowed women, its status was surprisingly legal. Her youthful self had not altogether approved, but by now she was long used to it, and what mattered was her collection.

Emma had made the library her life – and a good life it was.

Here she was in her element. Here she was taken seriously. It was where she was respected for her knowledge and her administrative ability. There was no one who knew the collection as she did, or who understood the esoteric cataloguing system. Although the trustees could be tiresome, as a private institution they were largely protected from the interference of the bureaucracy that seemed to dominate the lives of acquaintances who had gone into the public arena, or teaching, or any other profession, it seemed. And she was working with books. And people. Having grown up as a shy girl, she was surprised at how much pleasure she got from contact with the fellows: dusty old men looking at dusty old tomes, as her sister put it, but hiding a wealth of knowledge. They all shared a passion. This was their world too: a safe space in an often alien world. Emma looked fondly at the mostly white bent heads, almost like a mother hen, though most were considerably older than she was. Sometimes she felt that the wisdom of the classical world was held within these walls.

She knew most of the users of the library only by sight. It was a world in which silence ruled, with necessary conversations exchanged in a whisper or, if something more extended was required, they would retire to the hallway. In general, reservation slips and books could be exchanged with a smile. How she loved the stillness of this place! And the informality. Although fellows had to sign in, the club was small enough to dispense with the need for security badges for the staff. They were few in number and their faces were known.

The Antworthy Library had its origins in the private library of Dr Felix of the same name, a notable Greek scholar who, in the mid-nineteenth century, had bequeathed his collection on condition that it be housed together. So it formed the nucleus of what they had today. Of course, as a private club, they couldn't compete with the 120,000 volumes of the Institute for Classical Studies Library, but Emma liked to think that they had something unique to offer, and knew that the fellows appreciated the library's magnificent rococo ceiling and the appropriately stately building that housed it.

Although the building was of the eighteenth century, the interior was adorned not with the fripperies of the neo-classical age but with figures from the age of antiquity. Guarding the entrance were casts of stately statues of Roman emperors and, more pleasingly for Emma, at the entrance to the library, elegant busts of Socrates and Euripides. The Greeks were so much more refined. Although her own specialism was in drama, Emma drew succour from an environment imbued with the culture that had given it birth.

Of course the building was less grand than the Athenaeum and on the wrong side of the river, but it was in fact older and much in demand by curious-eyed visitors, particularly the library with its fine ceiling. Emma had insisted on limiting such distractions to Friday mornings. That was as much as she could do. The trustees were clear about the importance of keeping the club in the public eye. Despite some generous grant funding and a couple of individual and university bequests, the upkeep of such a building was a concern. Who knew where the next benefactor would be found?

Although the most precious volumes were in a climate-controlled annexe and had to be requested, in general there was an open access policy. Emma was proud of the availability of the stock to the fellows: that was what they came for, after all, and she was a great believer in the five laws of library science, which the Indian librarian Ranganathan had proposed in the 1930s, the first of which was "books are for use". But not off the premises. No book was to leave the building, unless a fellow could prove incapacity. And books had to be cared for. Only pencils were allowed in the library. And computers, of course.

Emma was pretty competent online but it gave her little pleasure. One of the original attractions of the job had been that it was relatively slow paced and low tech, but times had changed. Now keeping her job depended on her mastering a number of areas of new technology; that didn't mean she liked it. Her own house was a computer-free zone. Indeed, it was pretty much a gadget-free zone. No toaster or microwave. Certainly no dishwasher. She couldn't see the point. But at work she had to swallow her personal preferences. If the club wanted to attract younger readers, she knew that the presence of computers was inevitable. As it was, the library competed with the increasing online availability of digitally mastered material, which meant that people could access it from home.

It was hard to balance access to the widest possible materials with the natural preferences of the users. Sitting on a hard chair to access electronic periodicals wasn't to everyone's taste. Most of the fellows preferred to read a hard copy from the comfort of a leather armchair, but that was no longer always possible.

Some of the younger librarians that she met at conferences had quite different priorities and were keen to have the most up-to-date technology. But, even if they didn't see eye to eye on everything, it was always good to meet colleagues working in similar fields, and they seemed to respect her greater experience. Some had done their training online while working to pay their way. Emma heard how they struggled on low wages, living in little studio flats or travelling into the city from the outskirts. Thank goodness she had bought her little house before the prices rose so high. Living in London hadn't been an option for her then, any more than it now was for the younger generation. Looking at the state of the profession in general, she knew that they were all lucky to have jobs at all.

It was not often that Emma was called on to add to the collection. It was rare that a book of sufficient worth came to her attention, although occasionally, and most excitingly, a whole collection came up for sale, and sometimes the library benefited from a legacy of (not always suitable) books. In the old days, Emma had scoured the catalogues of specialist auction houses for possible acquisitions. Nowadays there were fewer opportunities and she hardly opened the trade press from one month to the next. Who needed another biography of Tacitus or exposition of women's role in the classical world? The library really had all it needed, and there was little room or money to expand. Her cataloguing skills were barely put to the test. Was she wearying of it all? Maybe it was time to go, to give way to someone younger and keener. But as soon as the thought entered her mind, her heart clamoured, "No!" This was her life.

Chapter 3

"Did you manage to renew *Birdsong*?"

"Yes, but they said this was the last time, so we'd better get on with it."

It was Friday, so Emma was in Bob's hall, taking off her jacket. She wore one out of habit, though it always seemed odd to go out of her door and into his, knowing that his house was just through her sitting room wall.

"Hard to imagine we'll finish it in three weeks. Maybe one of us will have to buy it."

"Well, let's see how it goes."

Bob's cottage was the twin of hers, except everything – stairs, bathroom – was on the other side of the house. Mirror-land. But, of course, the contents and feel of the houses were quite different. Bob was a man who had always loved working with his hands, and the results were everywhere to be seen – from the table to the bookshelves, groaning, as were hers, with books from every vintage. But he didn't pay the same attention to how things were arranged: the placing of the chairs, of ornaments and pictures on the wall. The lack of symmetry in his place irked Emma, but she had to remind herself that this was not her house but his.

The walls between the houses weren't thick, but the two of them were quiet souls, and didn't hear much of each other. And if Bob were in trouble, he knew he only had to knock on their common wall. As he had last year when he'd had the first of a series of little strokes. Emma had been round in a flash, sitting with him till the ambulance came, then going with him to hospital, staying until Alice, his daughter, relieved her.

He rarely talked about his daughter, but Emma knew she had a busy life in town. The two women got on well enough but when Alice came to stay, Emma stayed away. She felt father and daughter needed their time alone. Bob's main visitor nowadays was Shirley, well known to several of the older people in the village, who came in to care for him three times a day. So he had independence of a sort – and for the time being.

Emma had known Bob a long time, since he moved in over twenty years before. Now in his nineties, he was on the frail side, with sagging paunch and jowls, but in his deep eyes she could still see the keenness of his mind. He was someone who made her feel at home partly because to some extent he was a known quantity. Although his field was law not classics, he might have been one of the white heads from the club. And after all these neighbourly years, she was fond of him. Because of the age gap between them, she'd always thought of him as old, and now he really was. But he was no one's fool.

He took her coat. "Wine?"

"Mmm, thank you. Shall I get it?"

"Please. There's a bottle in the fridge."

Bob was one of the few people with whom she could talk about general books. Her days and conversation were dominated by the classical world, and the esoteric pleasures of reference enquiries. Strangely, most of the librarians she met didn't get much pleasure from reading. Working all day with the physical objects seemed to diminish the pleasure they got from reading them. They were like those orchestral players who on their days off couldn't bear to listen to music. Just imagine, what a deprivation!

Music was to Emma a life-saver that brought order and beauty into a chaotic world. She was not a practitioner and didn't claim to be a creative person. Unlike her sister, Denise, she had not shone at art. There had been a few juvenile poetic bunglings but on the whole she confined her literary efforts to essay-writing and now to reports. But as a bystander she was appreciative. Her musical taste, formed just as the Early Music Movement was coming into its own, was narrow and specific.

When period instruments became part of the mainstream, she prided herself on having been ahead of the crowd. Emma Kirkby was not only her namesake but her heroine. She loved the clear pure unwavering line that, had she been a believer, she might have said drew her up among the angels. Had she been given to flowery imaginings, she might have said that the almost impersonal nature of the sound, stripped bare of any emotional excess and shorn of vulgar vibrato, touched an answering chord in her soul. All she knew was that it brought her joy and lifted her on to a plane above the pedestrian concerns of daily life. It was only rarely that she allowed herself to be drawn into that other world. And then it was too important to be used as a background. When she listened, she gave it her full attention. The music and its performers deserved no less.

Bob's comforting sitting room was, as always, brightly lit to enable him to get around, and with a log fire giving out its inimitable cheer. Two glasses were already waiting on the table.

As Emma bent to pour the wine, some of it splashed on to the table.

"Careful. Anyone would think you'd had a snifter already!"

Emma laughed but she knew that it wasn't just carelessness. It had been happening more and more often lately – missing the glass, the coffee cup; finding that the plate or book she reached out for was a bit further to the right than she'd thought and a picture that seemed crooked became straight when approached from a different direction. To begin with, she had just sighed at the thought of another eye test – thicker glasses, more money – and finding the time to go.

At first, it was cataracts – all right, they were a bit worrying, but everyone said they were do-able, and so it proved. But then when her eyes started playing tricks, she was frightened and when Mr Holly – a man she trusted, an optician who knew her eyes – asked her to look at a grid of squares, and with her left eye the straight lines were no longer straight but wavy, she knew she was done for. It was a sure sign of macular degeneration. The dry sort, it turned out. Her niece had checked online; the optician and then the specialist at the hospital confirmed it. No cure. Gradual degeneration. It felt like the beginning of the end. Her eyes, the tools of her trade – without good sight she would be nothing, no job, no curling up at night with a good book.

Oh, she knew it was nothing compared to people who had MS, ME, cancer – nothing, except her whole way of life.

She hadn't told Bob. There was no point in upsetting him. He'd know soon enough, and she wanted to make the most of her Fridays while she could. They clinked glasses – *santé* – and caught up with each other's news. Their comfortable Friday routine.

In the old days they'd played Scrabble – it had been a delight to play with someone so evenly matched. But then Bob's word recall began to go, and it all became a bit of an ordeal. So they'd had to find another kind of entertainment, and reading was for both of them a pleasure. When Emma offered to read to him – "That way we can still have our evenings, and have a chance to share our pleasure in books" – Bob was reluctant to impose. He looked at her, scratching his chin.

"Are you sure, my dear?"

"Yes, of course. I'll enjoy it. I'd miss these evenings." Which was true but the offer was also a payback for all those years when Bob had come in to feed the cats when Emma was off on her visits to her sister. He couldn't manage it now, of course, so she phoned Sandra from across the road, who had a moggy of her own and was only too glad to come in after school and earn a bit of pocket money.

Emma swigged a little of her wine. "Shall we start?"

"Yes, my dear. If you're ready."

And Emma pressed on the handmade bookmark to open the book. "Oh yes, we'd just read about the fight at the factory.

Yes?"

Bob nodded. "Yes."

These days it was important to remind him of where they'd got to last time – she wasn't sure whether he remembered. So Emma read on, and the fire crackled, and they were both lulled by the sweet harmony of the room.

They took it in turns to choose a book, and Emma had chosen *Birdsong* because it was set during the First World War, a subject on all their minds as the centenary came and went, and she knew that for Bob it would have a particular resonance. They were only sixty pages in when Emma realised that it might be more to her taste than his. She wasn't surprised that it had been so well reviewed, but for her its strength was not so much in the much-praised scenes of war – it took a long time even to get to those and, besides, hadn't they had enough of that? – but in the love (or rather sex) scenes. To be frank, she wouldn't mind if they didn't finish it. She hadn't realised it was so long, and it was beginning to be embarrassing, reading such explicit passages out loud to a man, even if Bob and she had known each other forever, and she certainly didn't see him in *that* way.

After about half an hour Emma looked up, and saw that Bob was asleep. She shut the book and looked at him with a mixture of irritation and compassion. He would deny it, of course – *I was just resting my eyes* – but a slack jaw and open mouth told their own story.

It was time to go. He'd be mortified if he woke up to find her gone, so she knocked back the last of her wine, banged the glass on the table, and got to her feet. "Right, time I went home."

Bob jolted awake. "Yes, I was listening. Just resting my eyes."

Emma had a pact with Bob that she wouldn't read ahead. It was important that they experienced their chosen books at the same rate and at the same time. But this time she couldn't stop herself. Inside her own front door, she slipped off her jacket, and settled herself into an easy chair. She felt so involved in the developing love story that she cheated: she read on. She just couldn't help it.

As she got caught up in the sensual, sexual power of the writing, Emma was so aroused that she didn't know what to do with herself. What on earth was the matter with her? She, who had taken *Lolita* and *Lady Chatterley* in her stride, was behaving like a teenager.

But she knew what was "wrong": it was her "time of life", something that she'd started referring to as the Big M. (She seemed to have caught her mother's euphemistic turn of phrase.) And it was something that was turning her life upside down.

She had quite looked forward to the ending of the curse, being rid of all that messiness every month. She hadn't suffered much with her periods – just the odd cramp – nor with PMT (she wasn't the emotional sort) so she hadn't been too concerned about what was to come. She was used to the curse arriving on the dot, regular as clockwork, so when she realised after a few days that it hadn't come, she began to consider whether, in fact, she might be entering the menopause – she was that sort of age, after all.

She couldn't have envisaged being thrown into this kind of turmoil. She found herself less accommodating, on a shorter rein than normal. She who had always prided herself on her clarity of mind found that it was growing fuzzy round the edges, was invaded by emotions that she'd barely known existed. They kept popping up and distorting a perfectly rational state of mind. And then there were those appalling flushes that made her want to fling off her clothes. In the carefully controlled temperature of the library, there was no possibility of throwing open a window. She'd often felt a trifle warm after her bike ride, but nothing that a cool drink and a splash of water in the ladies wouldn't cure. What she experienced now was of a different magnitude: an out-of-control body that seemed at war with all that surrounded and constrained it.

HRT was not an option. Although Emma had discarded most of the beliefs of her Christian Scientist mother, she had inherited a distrust of medical intervention. As she'd always been healthy, the issue had rarely arisen.

At 11 p.m., Emma closed the book, yawning. She knew there was no way she could go on reading this out loud, least of all to Bob. What could she do? What excuse could she make?

In the end it was easy. The following week, she persuaded Bob that she had to take the book back, that its length prohibited their ever being able to get to the end of it – it wasn't really suitable for reading out loud. He made few complaints: they hadn't got very far with it anyway, and he happily agreed to move on to his next choice. No problem with Marcus Aurelius, whose wisdom lent itself to being savoured in small pieces. These short passages – equally if not more thought-provoking – were more suitable. And, as Bob's hearing deteriorated, it was getting to be a bit of a strain reading for any length of time. Bob had hearing aids, but hardly ever put them in, except when listening to the radio. Most of the time, as he said, there was nothing much to listen to. Emma was touched that Bob wanted to choose something from her world, even if it felt a bit close to work, but in fact *The Meditations* wasn't anything she'd ever studied. Too much of a cliché, perhaps. But no one could call it racy.

* * *

As Emma continued with the regular rhythm of her days, travelling by bike, train and bus, working at the library, going home to cats and her garden, she tried to put the strange image of dying flowers and a dark doorway out of her mind. She knew it had nothing to do with her, but for some reason it wouldn't go away. As she tried to push the subject away, an idea slipped in sideways. *How about…?* No, why would she? But the thought kept returning. She put her heightened imagination down to the general disturbance caused by Big M.

What she needed was a break.

Chapter 4

Her sister was at the bus station to meet her, with a beaming smile and a green streak in her hair. If she had any glimpses of grey, someone had done a good job of hiding them. Emma had never paid much attention to her own hair, but consoled herself that there was still more pepper than salt.

How good it was to see her. "Denise!"

Denise, surprised at the intensity of the hug, held her sister at arms' length, and studied her. "You okay, Em?"

Emma released herself, and wheeled her case to the car boot. It was a grey Vauxhall this time. Denise and Julian had campaigned for years for better public transport in their area, but had had to give in to using a car pool.

"Yes," said Emma stolidly, "I'm fine."

Denise climbed in behind the wheel. "Good journey?"

"Not too bad. A bit crowded. And someone on her phone the whole way. They always seem to forget they're in public."

"Mmm." Denise was adjusting her mirror.

Emma fastened her seat belt. "And the on-board lav was out of order, smelly – oh, but never mind. I'm here now."

"Yeah." Denise smiled at her and started the engine.

Emma sighed. "Sorry to go on. You okay?"

"Yeah, great, thanks. I'm afraid I'll have to work tomorrow afternoon."

"On a Saturday?"

"Yes, I've started a session once a week in the local community centre." Denise was a painter, and made ends meet by teaching evening classes and running workshops from time to time. "And Julian's going on the anti-austerity march." Emma kept quiet. Denise and Julian were forever going on marches, demonstrating against this or that in a seemingly random kind of way. Protest, it seemed, was a way of life.

Dorset was such a lovely county – so often bypassed in favour of the more popular Devon and Cornwall. Emma always enjoyed the drive through the byways to Denise's house, away from the coast, proudly alone atop a little hill. It seemed a shame to have chosen somewhere off the otherwise excellent bus routes, but she could understand the attraction of remoteness.

Emma took a deep breath, as she always did, on entering her sister's house and, as she always did, bid herself hold her tongue. The house was a shambles but it was not her business how they lived. Not that she was a cleanliness fanatic; she didn't enjoy housework either, she just liked things to be in their place. Apart from anything else, it was so time-consuming to have to *look* for things. It was a constant wonder to her how her sister got anything done. Without order, her own life would be chaos, especially with diminished sight. There would just be a jumble of objects, tasks and events. It didn't bear thinking about.

Denise kicked off her shoes; Emma bent down to unlace hers. Denise and Julian never wore shoes indoors, not to protect any carpet or floor but because they didn't like having their feet enclosed and, as Denise put it, without shoes they felt closer to the earth. From a room upstairs, Emma heard the strains of Julian's music. She didn't know what sort it was – pop? rock? She didn't know the difference, only that she didn't like it. But Julian was thoughtful; always when she stayed, he kept the volume down.

As usual, on a Friday night, they had the luxury of a takeaway. In Barleigh Common there was no such facility, and anyway Emma would have felt too guilty at the expense and self-indulgence. But, as that was what Denise and her partner did, she was free to enjoy her *nan* and chicken korma. She worried about eating chicken in a vegetarian household, but, as Denise airily said, as long as she didn't have to cook or prepare it, Emma could eat what she liked.

During the meal they caught up with each other's news.

"How's Posy?"

"Fine, I think. We haven't seen much of her. She's in London now, you know, in a shared house."

"Yes." Emma had meant to look her up, but rarely stayed in town after work. Emma liked her niece, who, despite her ridiculous name, was like her: the goggle-eyed studious type. Emma wasn't sure she would have coped with a more boisterous child.

She turned to her own affairs – her evenings with Bob and what was going on at work.

Denise helped herself to more rice. "When are you going to retire from that mausoleum?"

Emma clicked her tongue. "Denise, I wish you wouldn't."

"Come on, Em. You've got more life in you than sitting among a load of old statues and dodderers." She laughed. "Not much difference, now I come to think of it." Denise had always mocked her older sister. On a rare trip to London she had called for Emma at the club, and had not been impressed.

Being used to the silence both at work and at home, Emma wasn't much of a conversationalist, and was content to let the others talk. Once they'd cleared up, they sat with their coffee – or, in Emma's case, camomile tea – in the sitting room. Denise and Julian sat together on the settee, and Emma, disturbed by their open sexuality, looked away as Julian nonchalantly stroked her sister's breast.

Denise laughed and arrested his hand. "Oh, come on, Julian, we're embarrassing my big sister", and though Emma protested, it was true. Though she had always frowned on what she considered bad manners, she didn't remember such things troubling her so much before. Denise and Julian had no curtains up in their room. Apparently, they liked to gaze out from the cosiness of their bed at the moon and stars. Emma shuddered at the notion that they might be baring all for all the world to see.

"It's farmland, Em; no one can see. Don't be such a prude!"

But in the little attic guest room there was no such problem – just a skylight through which Emma could see the sky and the occasional flight of a bird. Strange, having been brought up in a north London suburb, that both girls, so different in every way, had chosen to live in rural surroundings. Her own country/city existence, straddling the two extremes, suited her just fine. She disdained suburbia and what she regarded had been the provincial tenor of her mother's life. Country or city, one or the other, not the blurred mediocrity of something in between.

Denise seemed happy with her Julian, though sometimes she treated him with a flippancy that made Emma wince. *Take care, Denise. Take care of your treasure while he's there.* He didn't seem to mind – indeed, seemed to delight in his partner's high spirits. Maybe he was just used to her sister's ways. Unlike Posy, who was embarrassed by her mother – well, Emma guessed that for children parents were always embarrassing. But there was some justification in Denise's case and Posy, now in her thirties, was a lot more sensible than her mother.

Emma supposed she would never understand the banter of conjugal life. Apart from some small glimpses of the lives of married acquaintances, she had no experience to go on. She marvelled at the interweaving of their lives. Denise was out a good deal – to her studio at the other end of town, and driving off a couple of times a week for her sessions at the art college. Julian worked partly at home and partly at a graphics design studio about ten miles away.

Emma had seen him that evening in a rather fetching soft black felt hat – they seemed to be back in fashion – she'd seen them out and about in London. "Fetching", now there was a word from the past, from her grandfather, in fact. For some reason, though he was long gone, she found herself thinking of him quite a bit these days. She hadn't known her father who had died before Denise was born. Or that was her mother's story. Emma, who had a misty memory of a tall male figure in her babyhood, wondered if he'd walked out on them, and her mother was too proud to admit it. There had been no point in asking her. She had always refused to say any more. Emma had never gone so far as to try and trace him, and Denise, with no memory of her father, showed no interest at all. As it was, their grandfather, a kindly soul of the old school, had been the dominant male figure as they grew up.

The following morning Emma got up at her usual time. The sky was bright and, even on holiday she was unable to stay in bed: restless legs and an equally restless conscience drove her to her feet. Wrapping herself in her dressing gown, she went down the stairs, taking care not to tread on the jersey and socks that had been cast off on her hosts' bed-ward journey last night. She longed to pick things up, put things straight, but knew that that would be a step too far. Their mess was nothing to do with her.

Emma made herself a cup of tea, secure in the knowledge that she would neither be disturbed, nor disturb anyone else. It was good to have had the bathroom to herself without worrying about being in the way of those with a later pattern to their day. She found a new packet of oats (bought specially for her, she knew; they didn't do breakfast), and made herself some porridge (with salt, of course: in that at least she was her Scots mother's daughter). As she served it up, Julian in a fleece and running shorts pottered into the kitchen. He brewed coffee for himself and Denise, then sat with Emma in sociable silence. He was a loping, broad-built man, some six inches taller than his partner. He had no perceptible accent but a laconic way of speaking that Emma supposed stemmed from spending his formative years in Australia.

Around ten o'clock, in leggings and a stripy tunic that barely reached the top of her thighs, Denise bounced into the room, hair tousled, her cheeks glowing with health.

Emma felt like a drab stick insect beside her colourful curvaceous sister. (*But you're the clever one,* she heard her grandfather say.) Denise was so much *younger* than her: she was "with it", or what was today's word? "Cool"? There were only a few years between them, but she felt they belonged to different generations. Maybe having children kept you young. Denise and Julian hadn't married – Emma knew her sister's view on the subject, and supposed that was their business – and Denise certainly hadn't had Posy christened. Emma liked to think of herself as open-minded but the traditional heart of her was pained. There were ways of doing things. Emma didn't know if her sister and Julian had decided not to have children or whether there was some problem. It was hardly a question she could ask. But in any case, Julian had always treated Posy as if she were his own.

At the sight of her sister, Emma was unable to stop herself. "Don't you think that's a bit young for you, Denise? Mutton, and all that?"

Denise laughed. "Oh, come on, Emma, I *am* young. Just because you're hanging on for your pension." She put a sisterly arm round her to mitigate the offence. "It's a lovely day. I'm not due at the centre till two, so I thought we might have a wander along the old railway track, if you like? And have a snack lunch at a pub, or something. It's a lovely morning."

Emma looked out of the window. Yes, for the time being it was. Denise could never imagine weather other than it was in the moment. If it was hot, she simply couldn't prepare for the cold: such a different temperature was beyond her imaginings. Emma, on the other hand, felt the cold, so tended to caution. She paid attention to the forecast and prepared accordingly.

Julian pushed his chair back from the table: "Okay, Denise, I'm off for a run now. All right?" and he kissed her on the nose before waving at them both. "Bye, guys, see you later." *Guys*! Emma supposed it was better than "girls" or "ladies". What did one say nowadays?

Once Julian had left the room, Emma returned to Denise's

question. "Yes, I'd like that. Thank you."

"You'll be able to amuse yourself this afternoon, won't you?"

Emma smiled and nodded. She liked this house, with its generous proportions. She particularly liked the window seat in the bay window, where on a fine day she could sit with a book, basking in the afternoon sun. Apart from the lack of feline companions, it was pretty well near perfection.

The walk was good, if a little muddy: Emma always enjoyed the opportunity to stretch her legs. And, as it turned out, it was warm enough to sit out with their ploughmans and beer. Dropped off at their house, Emma found herself a book, and sat, as she had promised herself, overlooking the slightly tired garden. She preferred coming earlier in the year when the garden was in full flow, and the riotous colour a better demonstration of Denise's exuberant talents.

All in all, it was a good weekend, with few undercurrents, and the Big M, for once, had been in abeyance. Emma felt refreshed, and returned to work with greater enthusiasm.

Chapter 5

On the first of the month, bedtime found Emma, as usual, stripped to the waist in front of the mirror. It was not a sight she enjoyed, but a chore undertaken after her mother's death from breast cancer, at 54 a year older than Emma was now. Indeed, she sometimes fancied that the image in the mirror was the face of her mother. Though Mummy had always said that Emma looked more like her father, she'd heard that as they grow older, women grow more like their mothers. Mummy had never worn glasses, of course. Even though she'd struggled to see much in later years, holding the paper close to her eyes, her faith told her they were unnecessary. She never seemed to have any problems in attracting men – in her youth by all accounts she'd been pretty popular. But in later life, her body had become flat, almost androgynous, and it was that broad and bony face that looked out at Emma now. She didn't like it one bit. Where was her womanliness, her femaleness? Now, more than ever, it seemed important to assert her femininity, even if the word was one that she associated more with her flighty little sister.

When her mother died, Emma, at thirty, had been the oldest of their immediate family, a role she found hard to accept. And, nearly twenty-five years later, she would soon be older than her mother had ever been. She tried not to be superstitious, but she had to admit a frisson at the thought, and realised that despite herself she was affected. Almost guilty.

By sight and by touch, Emma conscientiously examined her little-girl breasts. Not that her mother would have approved. In fact, it was an act of disobedience to a mother for whom all of the body had been supremely unimportant – but Emma had no intention of following her mother's path. If she was to get cancer, she wanted to know while there was still time to do something about it.

At least there wasn't enough of them to sag. As her palms brushed her nipples, she was embarrassed to sense, for the first time in many years, a flicker of excitement. Oh, God! How the Big M sensualised, sexualised everything. After all these years, it was awakening an urge that she'd thought dead. What a waste of energy. The rare occasions when she slipped her hands between her thighs were only in desperation, in denial, and in the dark – it took so much effort and brought with it an overwhelming sense of wrongness and guilt, however she denied it to her rational self.

Afterwards, she nearly always found herself in tears: from release, certainly, but also with an almost unbearable recollection of that short-lived flowering of her sexual self: a time remembered in her body, a time when she had seemed almost beautiful to herself, when almost anything had seemed possible.

Had her mother started the menopause? Emma couldn't remember her mentioning it – but, then, she wouldn't have done. She never complained about her ailments and wouldn't, in any case, have talked about anything so intimate.

Her mother's cancer had been caught late. No one knew whether her refusal of all treatment had hastened her end, or whether, at that point, it wouldn't have made any difference. At any rate it did mean that her consciousness was not dulled or altered by drugs; it meant that they were able to deal with the shock and say their goodbyes to a mother who was recognisably herself. She had been in pain, but remarkably calm and accepting: it was the family who had stormed at the dying of the light. Emma in particular had been in a state of shocked bewilderment. She'd been living with her, after all, and had been an intimate witness to the rapid decline from competent mother to a woman dying in her arms. She and Denise hadn't felt able to fight with her mother about treatment. She had been absolute in her refusal and there was a part of both girls that was persuaded by her steadfast belief in self-healing. It made her death the greater betrayal. Mum was not only dead, she'd been *wrong*, and Emma didn't know any more what she could believe. What else had her mother been wrong about?

Denise and she were sole beneficiaries and, along with Jenkins, the family lawyer, joint executors of their mother's Will. There was no question of Emma staying on in her mother's house. It would have chilled her and, anyway, Denise needed the money. Emma took compassionate leave but in truth the time was taken up not so much with grieving as in coping with the flurry of paperwork. Denise came up occasionally but she had her own family to think of so, as ever, it was Emma who took the brunt. And, anyway, it didn't really help to have Denise crying all over the place. It was a bit late now to feel guilty about the trouble she had caused.

Only when the death was registered, the funeral arranged, the headstone chosen, and the Will sorted, did grief and loneliness set in. Apart from a few months at university, Emma had never lived alone. The prospect was unnerving and, in odd half-hours snatched before and after work, the task of finding somewhere to live was almost beyond her. The search for an affordable London flat took her into smaller and smaller spaces in more and more distant places. As she gloomily contemplated the possibility of a dark little bedsit in a south-eastern suburb, Harry Jenkins came to her aid with a contact that led to where she was now. In a house of her own, in the country.

To begin with, she had been scared. Maybe it had to do with taking responsibility. The house was hers. There was no one to make choices for her. It was all a bit overwhelming when she thought about it – and she tried not to. Although coming back to this new home from work was a delight – it was hers; she had never had a home that was hers before, but she'd never lived in the country before, nor ever lived alone. She phoned Denise most evenings, then tried to find something to watch on

TV but after that there was nothing to fill the emptiness. Each night, though, she checked and double-checked the doors and the windows, when she got into bed she lay rigid, waiting for something to arrive.

Emma listened to the silence – and the noises. When she bought the house, she hadn't considered the wind. With little in the way, it blew across the fields opposite and hit the back of her house. She loved her shutters. She had had them stripped, and they gave her a greater sense of security – but they rattled. At night, in bed, the noises of a country house frightened her. These noises – so different from those of a double-glazed city flat, where the most that could be heard was the occasional row between neighbours, and the muffled sound of a siren – were here, close, in her house, posing a potentially intimate threat. And when there weren't any, she imagined them. Sometimes she slept with the radio next to her ear, but at some point it had to be turned off. The silence and the noises: they both had to be faced.

Chapter 6

To Emma's surprise, gardening had become a joy. It was important to her as an outlet for not only her physical energy but her practical intelligence. And, for someone who had no claim to creativity, it was a way of enabling something far more beautiful than she could ever have created herself. It was therapeutic too: pressing seeds or plants into the earth, digging, raking, rendering her bone-weary before a well-earned soak in a deep bath. A couple of hours in the garden brought not only the pleasure of nurturing the plants but induced a feeling of moral rectitude. Gardening was both a struggle and a reward, both penitential and uplifting. Every time a shoot appeared or a flower opened, she felt somehow that she'd earned it, deserved it.

Emma hadn't wanted a garden. When she bought the house, her heart had sunk at the sight of the oblong wilderness that began at the soon-to-be-painted back door. It was yet another chore. She spent the last of her "house" money on having the garden dug over and some turf delivered, then put it out of her mind while she addressed the needs of the house. But no sooner did she turn her back than, triffid-like, the weeds began to take over. The garden was a constant challenge to her orderly mind.

Having grown up on the second floor, Emma had no experience of gardens, except as a child at friends' houses, where they'd provided an opportunity to play out. As an adult, she'd envied others the opportunity to sit in the sun but had never given any thought to how anyone created such a space. She had no idea what to do, or what to grow.

She rang Denise. "What on earth do I do?"

"Plonk in a couple of shrubs that don't need attention, then you can think about the rest."

"I rather like that, oh, what do you call it? Clumps with the very high feathery white grass-like plumes."

"You don't mean pampas grass?"

"Yes, that's it. Why are you laughing?"

"As long as you don't put it in the front."

"Why ever not?"

"Umm, surely you know what that means?"

"No, what?"

"It means you're a swinger, up for a bit of 'ow's your father."

"What on earth do you mean?"

"Wife-swapping, standard signal."

Emma bristled. "Oh nonsense, Denise. Don't be so silly. And, in any case, as I've no one to swap, it hardly applies. Come on, what do you suggest?"

"What kind of soil do you have?"

"I've no idea."

Denise sighed. "Well, is it clay – cloggy, heavy – or sandy?"

"Well, it seems quite heavy, when I try to dig it."

"Right. Well, look up what suits that soil. Can't you get someone to start you off?"

"I've already paid out to get the place cleared. I can't afford anyone regularly."

Soon after that conversation, Emma found a battered copy of the Reader's Digest Encyclopaedia of plants in a local charity shop. It was ancient, but she couldn't imagine that plant information would go out of date. It was also very dense, and her heart sank. She scoured its pages for plants that were able to cope with her soil, took up lots of room and, most of all, were foolproof. She respected Denise's expertise, but didn't appreciate her sister's random approach to planting. Her own garden would be more formally colour-co-ordinated and planned.

One evening, after supper, Emma took her camomile tea into the sitting room, sat down with paper and pen, and made a list of plants that she'd vaguely recognised and that seemed to fit the bill:

Delphiniums

Lavender

Fuchsia

Dahlias

Rose – she'd have to have a look at the different varieties

Iris

Gladioli

Emma was a habitual list-maker: a list with relevant headings was the perfect way to keep the different strands of her life under control. As she sat, sucking the end of her pen and pondering her choices, Perky was washing herself by the radiator; Pinky asleep on the settee next to her. All was right with the world.

The following Saturday bloomed bright and cold – such a relief after all that rain – and Emma stuck to her resolution to go to the local garden centre. She parked her bike, walked through the automatic doors and took a trolley, realising it would probably mean that they would expect her to buy something. The family-run nursery was friendly and helpful. She had thought it might be a bit flaky but the bigger more established ones were full of furniture and other pricey accoutrements – all rather daunting and beside the point. Once she had explained her needs, a jaunty, square-jawed young man called Dell took her in hand. He paid no attention to her carefully researched list, waving the paper away with a gesture that spoke of a disdain of book-learning.

Leading the way, he said: "Come and see what we've got."

Pointing things out: "Well, there's Pittosporum for foliage" – was that what it was called? She particularly liked the one with small red leaves. "Ceanothus, Buddleia – the bees and butterflies like that, and for autumn colour you can't beat 'Pink Delight'."

Emma's trolley filled up in no time, mostly with plants she'd never heard of, but she recognised expertise when she heard it, and for once she had to trust her own response to the presence of the plants. It was not her usual way. Knowing nothing of the subject, she'd never taken much notice of different kinds of flower. If she didn't know the name, it held little interest for her. So it was almost with a sense of adventure that, in however small a way, she found herself straying from the boundaries of the known and familiar.

Thus began a tussle that was at first an irksome duty, a kind of drudgery, on a par with cleaning the house. Responsibility, the kind of good stewardship that she'd been brought up to observe. After months of back-aching struggle, Emma had had to confess herself beaten. However much she tried to impose her vision of shape and symmetry, plants would escape and have their way. They had a will of their own and eventually Emma had to admit defeat.

In time, as she accepted that plants would not be regulated, Emma began to enjoy their unexpectedness and find a different kind of satisfaction: both in the physical pleasure it gave her and in the sense that under her feet was burgeoning she knew not what. The mystery of the soil. Although she had her failures, most of her efforts brought some sort of result either straight away or, in her rusty imagination, would do so in the future. She liked the fact that gardening was about planning: for next spring, or a few years' time. It was the one time when the future seemed more expansive than the present. Maybe the fact that there was little else to plan for as you got older was the reason garden centres were full of old people. Emma knew she didn't have the flair of her green-fingered sister, but a combination of application and rooting powder seemed to do the trick. To her surprise, Emma now began to enjoy herself.

Work in the garden became part of the pattern of her days. Living in the country, she was more conscious of the seasons, closer, really, to everything that happened. She found that it brought out of her a different, slower, rhythm: a good counterbalance to the pressures of work and city life, the demands of ever-speedier communication. The problem with commuting, though, was that between October and March, even if she caught the earliest possible train, by the time she got home, and had fed herself and the cats, it was dark. It meant that it was generally April before she could get out into the garden during the week. In the growing season her weekends were pretty full on.

Emma was meticulous about wearing gloves in the garden. She couldn't allow her nails to get ingrained with dirt: it wouldn't do in a job like hers, where hands were on display. And, anyway, she quite liked her hands: her long slim fingers were one of her few vanities. For hacking down the shrubs, then carving them up into manageable pieces for the compost, she had bought thicker gloves, but the heavy digging was beyond her strength, and she hired Vince from the village to come and do it. He was a beefy taciturn man, born and bred in the locality, and they suited each other well, working away with a nod and just a fraction of a smile at the end of the day.

But she had to admit to the random nature of her "success". Apart from her own activity, there were so many elements – literally – that contributed to it. Water, earth, air; wind, weather and soil, not to mention the random nature of the creative spirit. Flowers popped up quite unexpectedly, not at all where she'd carefully judged their height and colour to be most appropriate. Self-seeding disrupted the most considered of her plans. Seduced by the pink frilliness of a poppy, she hadn't the heart to uproot it. She must be getting soft. Whatever, it was good to be in touch with living, growing things after a day spent among the dead and, as Denise would no doubt say, those well on the way to becoming so.

She found that constant attention made her plants flourish. She knew the truth of the old saying, "The best thing you can give your garden is your shadow", but was that really what she wanted for her garden? She knew it meant her presence but it wasn't a phrase that she liked. As a child she'd been scared of her shadow, that dark entity that pursued her everywhere and, however silly it was, as an adult she still avoided looking at it, and couldn't believe that that looming presence could ever be benign.

Emma was not a courageous person. Her mother had called her a "timorous wee beastie", an affectionate enough term, but Emma was harder on herself. She remembered with shame how she stood by when she saw a small girl at school, her arms protecting her head, cowering beneath the taunts of the bullies. It reminded her of a stricken bird being surrounded and pecked to death. But Emma had done nothing. If her sister had been there, she would have flown to the rescue.

Denise had always been the fearless one, shouting *scaredy cat* when Emma refused to climb over a wall, or follow her up on to a higher branch. As the older sister, it was humiliating. But Emma told herself that she was sensible: she could see what might happen, and knew that if it did, she would be the one to bear the brunt. As the first child of a single mother, Emma had learnt early to take responsibility. And that conscientiousness had liberated Denise, given her licence, provided a shield behind which anything might happen. Which it did.

Denise started playing up when she was about fourteen. By the time Emma went to college, her sister was completely out of hand. Without Emma to keep an eye on her and to act as a mitigating bridge with their mother, Denise was unmanageable, keeping what Mum disparagingly called "bad company", drinking and staying out till all hours. At least that was what Mum said in her letters. It was quite a relief when Denise got a place at art school in Brighton and although Mum worried about her, she was at least out of her hair.

Denise was half-way through her second year when she came home to announce that she was pregnant. Emma had never forgotten the row that erupted. The wrath of their mother was terrible to behold. She had confronted her younger daughter in the sitting room, just as Emma was on her way in. Seeing what was about to happen, she turned on her heel and made for the safety of her room.

"How," she heard blasted from behind her, "could you be so irresponsible? How could you do such a thing?"

"Irresponsible? What about you? You brought us up on your own. We've turned out all right."

"Yes, with great difficulty. Couldn't you see how hard it was for me? And I didn't choose it. You can't help death."

Or abandonment, thought Emma as she mounted the stairs. She couldn't help feeling that a lot of their mother's anger was not about Denise.

It was only in the evening that Emma had got a defensive sister to herself. "Wow, that's a poser. Are you all right?"

"Yes, thanks. But I'm getting out of here. I might have known that Mum wouldn't understand."

At least, Emma stuttered, Denise hadn't – she'd decided to keep it.

"Oh," said Denise with her customary bluntness, "I did wonder about an abortion. But I so love living things. And to give birth to one myself: what a privilege. A miracle really." She shook her hair. "Of course, it's been an awful shock," she confided. Not only to her, Emma thought. What about the rest of us?

But she battled on. "But you could do with some support. What about the father?"

Denise turned those fierce eyes on her. "What about him?"

"Have you told him?"

"Yes. He didn't want to know. Said he was too young for that kind of responsibility. Bastard. Anyway" – she took a swig of her coffee – "I'm off. See you."

No more was said on the subject, then or later. Emma never did find out anything about the father. Rather like their own, it was as if he'd never existed. But Denise's daughter had a right to know. Had she asked? Would she try to find out? It wasn't surprising that during her pregnancy Denise had stayed out of their way. But when Posy arrived, they all fell in love with her, and even Mum was reconciled.

Posy! What kind of a name was that? "Posy," said Denise dreamily. "Makes me think of flowers. She'll be my little flower." Rose would have done, thought Emma, or even Daisy. But even if she wasn't a flower, she was a lovely little girl. She couldn't help her name, after all, and she was adorable.

"You know, Em," Denise had turned to Emma with that familiar earnest look, "everyone has a flower identity."

"Oh?" said Emma warily.

"Yes, it's not your favourite flower but the one that represents you. Not just the blossom, but the whole plant, the entire flower of our being: the petals, the stem and above all, perhaps the roots."

Despite herself, Emma was impressed. Goodness, little sister, hark at you. Amazing what you can find on the internet.

"I'm a camellia," Denise dreamily went on: "the flower of love. And you," she said consideringly, "you could be an iris: cool, elegant and self-sufficient."

You mean inhibited, thought Emma. But, despite her scepticism, she had never forgotten that conversation, and occasionally, when she met someone, a flower image popped unbidden into her head.

Johnny, for instance, Johnny resembled nothing so much as a sunflower.

Chapter 7

It was a year after her mother's death, when Emma was emerging from the grieving process, that they had met. Even with his shock of corn-gold hair, Johnny was too lanky to be conventionally good looking, but he was carefree, and had about him a life-enhancing lightness of being. Tall, gawky, with little to show except a brilliant crown, always turned towards the sun.

As they got to know each other, Emma worried that Johnny had rather more in common with Denise, who was younger, prettier and at that time unattached. In fact, Emma had once wondered – no, don't go there. That way madness lay. She had been worried about introducing them, but it was apparent, from the word go, that, however unbelievably, it was her that he loved. Even when she'd recovered from the astonishment, it seemed wrong, somehow, to be so happy.

As a family they had never gone in for touching, not even the occasional hug. To Mum the body was a matter of indifference; only the spirit mattered. So when Johnny first took Emma in his arms, she froze in embarrassment, and averted her head.

But Johnny was tender. "Darling, it's all right. Look at me. Come on, look at me."

And when she looked into his warm brown eyes, the tension began to seep from her body. That body, never touched, never acknowledged, began, almost despite itself, to respond. They took it slowly, and to her amazement the feel of her body, and of his, began to give her pleasure. She was ashamed – and Johnny was touched – by her inexperience.

Emma didn't see a great deal of him. He worked long and erratic hours, often at night in order to connect with the working hours in Australia or Hong Kong. He also seemed to travel a lot. When she met him, he'd just come back from Beijing. She never really understood what he did. Something to do with IT. She couldn't understand why working with IT would involve travel. When she asked him, he smiled and said, "Honestly, darling, if I tried to explain you'd be asleep in no time." When she pressed him, Johnny squeezed her thigh and said, "Come on, I don't want to talk about work. I have enough of that the rest of the time." It was the nearest he ever came to patronising her. But she didn't mind, and didn't really care what he did. What was real was how they were together. She was content to talk of music and beauty and of her work to someone who genuinely wanted to know. Not that they always agreed. His musical taste was for a wider canvas and what he called a more full-blooded sound. For his sake she had tried to listen to Mahler, but found her fingers twitching for a blue pencil to put an end to his long-windedness. And at Wagner she drew the line.

And they talked of love. Not in public. She felt strongly that their affection was for their eyes only, not for public view. Johnny laughed at her primness and graciously succumbed.

Johnny was full of ideas: Wimbledon, Tate Modern, maybe they could take a boat out one weekend. He sometimes hired one in Poole; maybe they could go over to Cowes. Emma didn't swim and, apart from a childhood day trip to Calais, she had never been on the water, but if Johnny wanted to, that was fine by her. With him, anything was possible.

Life opened up. It was as if Johnny held the key to a more expansive universe, where Emma saw, heard, felt, everything more keenly, where she became aware of opportunities that had been hidden from her in her little closed-in world. Her mother's life had been narrow – Emma saw that now – and she even began to understand a little of her sister's rebellion. Life was good; the sun shone: she felt as if she were shining with it. The joy of Johnny's presence opened her heart and eyes but it wasn't just his sunny attitude to life – it was the effect of being loved. Before Johnny (BJ), and after (AJ), her Saturday mornings were spent in catching up on chores – the washing, shopping, cooking and cleaning. For that brief spell he had shown her that it could be different. Meeting for coffee and croissants in Soho, then on to a CD shop and to the British Museum to look at the drawings (for him) and the manuscripts (for her). Only after that would they reluctantly part and catch up with their chores.

She didn't mention him at work but people noticed the spring in her step.

"Met someone, have we?" said the post boy, Ken, who had a keen eye for such things. And despite Emma's blustering denial, no one was taken in. But for once Emma didn't care. Let it show; let it shine. She was happy.

And being with Johnny rid her of fear. It was as if his advent into her life helped her emerge into the bright light of day, as if his presence drained the very possibility of fear. One afternoon, as she sat reading in her favourite garden chair, Johnny approached from the house behind her and laid his hand on her back. As she looked up, the first thing she saw was his shadow on the grass, and in that moment she knew that a shadow could be beautiful.

She had never sought to recover that enchantment. By now, so many years later, the pleasure of touch was a long-distant memory. There was no point in seeking to recapture a dream, least of all now, in her ageing menopausal self. That butterfly had had its day. Any replacement, like the grossness she saw all around her, would be ugly.

The image of a butterfly brought to mind that impossibly glamorous dress of brilliantly striped taffeta. How had she ever been persuaded to buy it, let alone put it on? The dress was long gone to Oxfam, but was forever captured in a photo not discarded but hidden away, a little picture at the edge of her memory, glimpsed out of the corner of her eye. She couldn't bear to look at photos from that time. It was too painful. The album of photos, from a pre-digital age, was gathering dust in a box under her bed.

There was a time when things were different. There was a time... But it was a time that didn't bear thinking about. A time that was shut away in the box along with the photos.

Chapter 8

After work, Emma usually went straight home. She rarely had a reason to linger in town, and it was some time since she'd visited the scenes of her student youth. She'd always liked the area round Wigmore Street, so it was no hardship to do an errand for Bob, and pick up a lumbar support from an old-established specialist back shop that Bob remembered and trusted from his more mobile days. Emma could have bought it online (Bob, of course, didn't have a computer) but, being wary of giving out her financial details, she preferred to go in person.

It was a clear bright day and there was time to spare before her train went so, with a package tucked into her bag along with her helmet, Emma decided to stroll around the local streets. Harley Street, Wimpole Street, centres of medicine for the affluent. She wasn't likely to use their professional services, but how she enjoyed the spacious symmetry of the streets and, even through the inevitable scaffolding and netting, the stately elegance of the Regency buildings. Although she rarely sought it out, fine architecture, a word that from the Greek meant literally "the weaving of a higher order", had always been a pleasure, a soothing reminder of harmony in the rough and tumble of London life.

Not that the architecture was uniform – far from it. Some of the buildings were faced with painted stucco; others bared their red brick; some were flat fronted, others with bow or squarish window projections. Emma was even more surprised at the amount of greenery. Carefully tended window boxes and hanging baskets – even three hanging from a wrought iron arch in front of one of the front doors. Someone, she saw, had planted marigolds and pansies round a couple of the trees in the street. It was hard to remember, in the bustle of suits and mobile phones, that this was not just a working area, but one where people lived.

Absorbed in her surroundings, Emma wandered further north than she'd intended and, as she approached Euston Road, she was arrested by a large sculpture on the wall of one of the buildings. A seemingly random arrangement of circular terracotta tiles, it stood several metres high. To the side was an information plaque with a picture of a sunflower. Ah, yes, now she could see it. The sculpture was a representation of a sunflower head. But the title was "Fibonacci Flip". Fibonacci, and a *sunflower*?

The word "Fibonacci" was familiar – you couldn't forget a word like that – but she couldn't put her finger on where she'd heard it. As for "flip", it sounded like a dance. Ah, Fibonacci sequence, that was it – it was something that had been bandied about at university by classicists of the mathematical persuasion. Since maths was not exactly Emma's strongest point, she hadn't taken much notice.

But wasn't Fibonacci something to do with the golden ratio? That *was* significant. The whole idea was such a pleasing one, one that gave her orderly mind a deep sense of satisfaction. Proportionality, symmetry, the qualities of the golden mean, these were the basis of her love of Greek and Renaissance art. Even if her own specialism and career had moved her in a different direction, it was good to be reminded of those early years of study. And, now she came to think of it, hadn't Plato written something about it in relation to the structure of the cosmos? In the *Timaeus*, wasn't it? – not one that she'd read, and her aversion to maths had blanked it out.

It went against the grain to believe that a sequence of numbers could have anything to do with the natural world but, curiosity stimulated by the sculpture, Emma went online in her lunch break. And there she found it. The seed head of a sunflower was famous, apparently, as an example of Fibonacci in the natural world. Really? As she looked further, she was amazed to discover the notion that nature has a numbering system, an order underlying everything. That world that she had fought with and found so unruly had, it seemed, an innate order of its own. Not exactly obvious. But, according to what she read, everything that grows confirms its innate proportionality: the arrangement of the heart of a sunflower, of leaves on a stem, of branches on a tree – all unconsciously maximising light. That the beauty of proportionality could lead to such efficiency. Now there was a thought!

Emma didn't begin to understand how it all worked, but she started to consider plants with a new level of wonder and respect. With a certain degree of self-consciousness, she took the time to examine individual flowers: the number of petals, the centres – so often densely packed like a miniature sunflower head; she saw how even the flower head of a chive plant was seemingly made up of lots of little flowers, each with its own centre.

That there should be this one sequence that brought together her twin worlds was overwhelming. It was an affirmation, if she had needed it, of the importance of pattern, of order. Even more, it suggested an underlying and overarching principle to the whole of life. It was the kind of ground of being that, while rejecting her mother's beliefs, while not finding in any conventional religion anything that answered her need, she had sensed and envied in her mother's faith.

Considering flowers – the delphiniums, the asters, the Michaelmas daisies – with more concentrated attention, Emma marvelled at the combination of similarity and diversity. It was almost – almost – enough to make her believe in a creator God, or some kind of unifying life force. Before she could be quite overcome, she steered herself away from such romantic notions and retreated to the safer certitudes of order, patterns and symmetry that Fibonacci represented.

In the meantime, she would grow sunflowers! It was the least she could do. In fact, she wondered why she hadn't thought to grow them before. Maybe she'd been put off by the rather twee images of Van Gogh's paintings or because her image of the real thing was not, as was increasingly frequent, of massive heads reduced inappropriately into vase-length bunches. She was a bit disgruntled at their increased popularity, demeaning to her eye the statuesque pride of those golden giants in fields stretching as far as the eye could see. For her they were special. But increasingly they were being grown in gardens – apparently they were tough, remarkably easy to grow and suited to any soil. More to the point, they were such a symbol of hope and light, and such a reminder of her Johnny. *Helianthus*. Flower of the sun.

In general, Emma stuck to perennials – she didn't want to have to think of new things every year – but, in this instance she was content to make an exception, happy that each spring would bring a reminder. When she asked the man in the garden centre, he shook his head. "Sunflowers? Oh, they just shoot up and flower, and then," with a dismissive hand gesture, "they're gone." Emma had closed her eyes on the pain of that image. But, when the man had left and she came to examine the packet of seeds, she saw that the seeds could be used either for eating or putting back in the ground, that flowering could be prolonged by deadheading and, reading further, that sunflowers have roots that grow deep and spread wide. Maybe they were not so ephemeral after all.

Chapter 9

Emma's ingrained privacy extended to her work. Friendly with her colleagues, feeling the comfort of being part of a solid organisation, she did not delude herself that she was one of them. Apart from Trevor, who had been there even longer than her, she was the oldest and, whatever people said, age did matter. They had all grown up in different generations with cultural references that meant nothing to the others. She herself let out very little. Cottage, cats, sister – there was not much else to say.

So on 14 October as all the staff were gathered as usual for their morning coffee break, when Marilyn from Accounts appeared in the doorway bearing a glowing smile and a candled cake, Emma was astounded. How did she know?

It turned out that the cake was for Marilyn's own birthday, which fell on the same day as Emma's, and so on that day the year before had begun a tradition of alternating responsibility for the celebration. So too began an unlikely friendship, slow-burning as was to be expected between two such different women whose paths rarely crossed in the line of work, but less so because of Marilyn's irresistibly bubbly and social nature. Her husband was Greek, apparently: they'd met when Marilyn had been on holiday in Crete with her parents, and he'd been working in his uncle's restaurant. "Dancing, plate throwing, the lot!" Marilyn recalled with delight. Emma shuddered at the thought. Was that what her beloved Greek culture had come to?

Marilyn was what Emma's mother would have called vulgar. She was a strange sort of friend for Emma to have, but in truth Emma rather enjoyed her cheerful flashiness. Twenty-something, and eight months pregnant, she'd been at the library for about eighteen months. Given the staid nature of the club and its members, she was a rather surprising appointment, but

Emma gathered that she was some sort of connection of one of the trustees. A working-class girl, she had something of a gift for maths, and was warm, cheerful and, at the moment, extremely large. In fact, she was generally plump, which meant that the bump of her pregnancy seemed not so much like an addition as an integral part of a well-rounded body. In Denise's terminology, a peony in full bloom. Even before her pregnancy she'd threatened to spill out of her sober work clothes. Outside work, Emma knew, Marilyn's image was rather more outlandish and would have shocked Trevor and the other more conservative members of staff.

As Marilyn's pregnancy advanced, Emma was increasingly aware of the younger woman's expanding body. It was partly that, as the only other woman in the club, Emma was someone for the younger woman to confide in.

"Come on, Em," she would say, taking Emma's reluctant hand, "feel it. You can feel him kick." She wasn't just generally friendly, she genuinely seemed to like Emma, who, despite embarrassment at the excessive bodily contact, was flattered by her unexpected warmth. She would really miss her when Marilyn took her maternity leave.

At the end of one rainy October day, as they met in the ladies, Marilyn held the sides of her belly and sighed. "Oh, God, I'm sick of waiting; I wish my waters would break."

Emma had an image of her friend's belly as a pricked balloon with water gushing from below. And then turned away to hide her blush at the raw physicality of the image. What was the matter with her? Suddenly, as the heat coursed through her, the straitjacket of library rules and the sedate behaviour of those sitting there became well-nigh intolerable. She longed to shout, make a noise, up-end the tables, shock them all out of their complacency. As if all the stifled emotions, the swallowed words, all the pain, had been squashed into a body that felt full to bursting. It was hard to believe that the moment would pass, even harder to hang on until it did, to show the bland face of her usual composure while sweating and bursting at the seams. She was not herself. The real Emma was unruffled and composed. She had deportment, carried herself with dignity. This was all so shocking and *undignified*.

Back at home, shaking the rain from her umbrella, Emma felt an abdominal shift and then, as if in sympathy with her equally hormonal colleague, the blood gushed at last with the power of an established period. As she ran to the bathroom to mop herself up, Emma was overwhelmed by a sense of physical relief. And more than that. If she was still bleeding, did that mean she was still fertile? She caught the thought. What did she mean? Why should she care? It was not as if children had entered her consciousness for more than fleeting moments over the years. She recalled Plato's dictum that all human beings are pregnant physically and spiritually and that when we reach our prime, our nature desires to give birth. Goodness knows what she could give birth to. No, uncomfortable though it was, Emma had to admit that what reassured her was the confirmation that she was still a sexual being, that she still had a spark, hadn't yet become one of the invisible.

* * *

When Emma woke the following day, the thought struck her that she'd never lived. She didn't know why it should come to her at that moment, at the age of 53. No anniversary, no significant date, just waking with sudden clarity to an overview of an empty life.

As she travelled to work, she felt cocooned in loneliness. Emma saw some of the regulars chatting on the train, but had never got further herself than smiling and saying hello. What did they find to talk about? They didn't know each other. But who could she talk to? She had no friends to speak of. Bob was a dear, but not someone with whom she could share anything intimate. Nor was Marilyn – they were too different in every way. And, for all their affection, she and Denise had little in common. Apart from Johnny, who had there been? Her former neighbours, Rita and Louise, had been good friends, but when they moved away, they'd lost touch. She wondered if they'd still get on. She was on Christmas card terms with a couple of UCL friends but although they always wrote about getting together in the New Year, with each year that passed, the likelihood seemed more remote. Alice had married – *just a small family affair* – and Sonia had gone travelling. Emma read their news with a detached interest and no sense that it had anything to do with her. Neither of them had continued in the world of classics – she seemed alone in upholding the passion that they once had shared.

Emma didn't know why she had so few friends. Come to think of it, she was a bit like her mother in that. Other people seemed much more sociable. Denise, for instance, was the sort of person who would talk to anyone – strangers in the park or at the bus stop – probably whether they liked it or not. When Emma stayed with her, people rang, even occasionally dropped in, although Denise said most of her contacts were on social media. Where did people get all those Facebook friends? Or all those friends they phoned as they walked down the street? Not that Emma had any wish to go on Facebook or anything like it, but she still wondered where she was going wrong. Was she so hard to like? She knew quite a lot of people, could even say that the club was her community – all those men she'd seen over the years, in many cases every day. At one level, they knew each other. They just didn't need to speak.

But in a different part of herself, Emma knew that she did. She needed a more vocal connection. Ordinariness. Chat. It didn't help to blame Big M for her misery. Whatever the cause, it was still how she felt. Her solitude, normally so precious, suddenly felt like an emptiness. Just a lack, an absence.

Part of the cause of her disequilibrium, she knew, came from thoughts of her mother's death at a similar age. And from intimations of retirement. From a casual suggestion at her last staff review to something that felt more like a not-so-gentle pressure to go. And with the state of her sight, she was unlikely to have much choice.

Emma had taken to picking up little bits of cotton and paper from the carpet, as if to prove to herself that her sense of sight was still there. She found herself looking at her house with new, diminished, eyes, making an imprint on her brain of how and where things were so that, when it had to, memory might take the place of sight. Memory. And touch. She started to notice how things felt, wandering round the house, sometimes in the dark, using touch as a way of navigating her way as practice for when she would have no choice. It would help that she already had such an orderly life – she knew where things were, because she always put them there. It was a practice bred in her bones. As a child, she'd watched her grandfather with his carpentry tools, each one slotted into its special place. He could always reach out and, without looking, pick out the right one.

Emma cast a critical look at her lighting. Maybe she could do with a better reading lamp and, much as she hated them, a fluorescent tube in the kitchen. It was a long time since she'd had any work done on the house. She'd ask Bob, and perhaps Vince, if they knew anyone who could do it. Maybe she would need rails to hold on to. Maybe she'd become unable to continue living independently; maybe, like Bob, she'd end up with a carer.

As the maybes became more extreme, she pushed her morbid thinking aside, propelled herself out of her chair, went in search of Pinky, and held her, squirming, to her chest. Thank God for the cats.

Retirement – how she hated that word. It wasn't the money.

They had reassured her that she would get her full pension, quite considerable now that she had been there nearly thirty years. Thirty years! Although she certainly wouldn't miss the commute – the standing, the squashing and the body odour, not to mention signal failures and leaves on the line – she loved her work and being with others. She liked dipping her toe in the big city world, from which her village and little cottage were a refreshment. Her London life, she felt, gave her an edge, made her feel sophisticated – not just a country cousin. But retirement would be just that – alone with the cats, shrinking her life into that of a little old spinster in a little old village. What a cliché! Nothing to tell one day from another. Of course she could go down to London, but it wouldn't be the same. She wouldn't belong. She wouldn't have her domain.

Above all, she'd be lonely. Although she spent much of the day without speech at the club, she was surrounded by people, people who valued her as a person and what she had to offer. In retrospect, she wondered about her decision, all those years ago, to move to the country and live alone, a decision that, looking back on it, seemed uncharacteristically courageous, not to say foolhardy, but at the time had seemed her only choice.

Without a car, retired life would be pretty limited. She hadn't realised how many of the amenities of her daily life were reliant on her being in London: cash points, 24-hour shopping. She had her bike of course but what about when/if she were no longer able to ride it? As it was, if she had a puncture, she had to call in favours.

Retirement would be a closing in, a step nearer death, a little death in itself. She could almost hear Denise say: *From one near-death experience to another!* The running commentary in her head, her inner monologue, was often punctuated by comments in her sister's voice. Less so, now, her mother's which had faded from her mind. And, as for Johnny's... it was long gone.

That doorway and the flowers stayed with her. How strange

it was. She'd seen any number of these roadside shrines. They had always jolted her, as an intimation of tragedy, but they had never had the impact of this one. Maybe it was because the flowers were hand-picked, felt so personal to whoever had laid them there, that it felt, irrationally, personal to *her*. Maybe it was because the dark mystery reminded her of other feelings of disquiet; long buried, and now that a protective skin of forgetfulness had been stripped away, what was revealed was a raw and deep-rooted uncertainty.

It wasn't, she knew it wasn't, about Johnny, but it felt as if it was.

What could she do? Emma knew she wouldn't rest until she had put down a marker of some sort. Until she had *done* something. The germ of an idea that she'd had some weeks before grew in her until it crystallised into a plan. As she got into bed that night, she turned on her side and snuggled down in its warmth with a feeling of satisfaction. At last there was something she could do.

Chapter 10

The following morning, Emma got up with a sense of purpose. She always enjoyed the early morning routine. She set an alarm but nearly always woke before it, and took a little time before pushing off the bedclothes and greeting the by now vocal cats. Switching on the light – she did not draw the curtains until she was dressed – drawing on her dressing gown, visiting the bathroom, emptying her bladder and the hot water bottle, splashing her face with cold water (so good for the skin), and taking care not to trip over Pinky and Perky as they accompanied her downstairs. Drawing back the heavy sitting room curtains, opening the shutters, switching on the kettle and radio. Opening the house and herself to the day. At weekends she took the radio to bed with a cup of tea and let the sound of voices wash over her as she luxuriated in an extra hour in bed.

On this morning, when Emma pulled up the kitchen blind, it revealed rays of sun glinting through the trees and a faint haze, bearing the promise of later warmth. Even through the closed door she could hear the early morning chatter of the birds. With a soft feline caress around her ankles, life was good. It was hard, on such a day, to believe in death.

Nonetheless, she held true to her purpose. She took the secateurs from the kitchen drawer, and went down the garden path. She walked past the reliable chrysanthemums, past the blood-red glory of the peonies and on to the last of the sunflowers, standing proudly, their faces towards the rising sun. Stooping, she clipped three of their long straight stems near the branch of the stem. She considered the large and striking flower heads. Really, the Fibonacci sculpture had not done them justice. There had been nothing of their sunny glory or dark centre with its tiny glistening silver points. Like tiny droplets or pinheads in a cushion of velvet darkness.

Back at the house, she laid the flowers on the draining board before running up to the bathroom for some cotton wool. Wetting it under the tap, she wrapped it round the stems and carefully placed them in a little plastic bag, before attaching them across the basket of her bicycle.

As Emma sat on the train, holding the flowers between her knees, she was nervous. Her proposed intervention that the night before had in some indefinable way seemed momentous and meaningful, in the morning light seemed excessive, even intrusive. At Victoria, with the flowers in her arms, she struggled to release a bike from its docking station and, without a basket to put them in, she hugged the flowers to her as she rode carefully to her destination. At the door of number 37, she gently laid the three stems on the ground, leant the bike against a lamp post and, peering nervously around her, began to untie the bundle of dead flowers.

"What are you doing? What the *hell* are you doing?"

Another Boris bike came to a screeching halt beside her, and a tall girl with wide eyes and streaming red hair shouted in her face.

Emma shrank.

"How dare you? Messing with the flowers! Do you know why they're there?"

Emma nodded and gulped. Only too well. "I was bringing, I noticed, I have these in my garden, thought it would be nice..."

"*Nice!*" The girl could hardly contain herself. "Why? What business?" Breathless and almost as incoherent as Emma, she stepped off her bike, and brushed copper hair away from her face.

"I'm sorry. I had no right, I know. I just felt..."

"But *why?*"

Yes, why? Emma was at a loss. They stared at each other, stricken.

"Sorry," Emma whispered again and fled, abandoning the

flowers, both the live and the dead.

In a nearby street, she sat down on a low wall and shook. She tried to breathe. What had she been thinking? What on earth had she thought she was doing? She pulled her mobile phone from her bag and with trembling fingers pressed some numbers.

"Trevor? It's Emma. I'm sorry but I won't make it in today. I started out but my migraine's really bad now – I can hardly see. I'll have to go home. Yes, thanks, I will. Sorry to let you down."

So back she went, the way she had come, averting her eyes as she passed the doorway. Head down, blindly dodging chuggers and leaflets proffered by outstretched hands. Back to the station, out of the wind, hoping she could hold on. Sitting on the train, fighting to contain the tears behind her lids. From Leatherhead she cycled with little control and dangerously bleary eyes, and let herself in to her private space. Why hadn't the girl been wearing a helmet? Surely she, of all people?

Nicola

Chapter 11

I couldn't believe it when I saw that old biddy standing there, that precious bouquet in her hands. Actually, when I looked, she wasn't that old, just dressed and acted like something out of the last century. Was she mad? What the hell did she think she was doing?

I'd gone there that third time to put some new flowers there myself. The first ghastly time I'd been too shocked to notice anything except a dirty beige door, a very ordinary terraced house, and the police tape across the pavement. I'd needed to go back. The second time, the tape had gone, and I nearly missed it.

I could only go after work, or at the weekend. As it was nearer work than home, I decided to go one evening. It was an awkward journey, but a bike would do it. What a blessing those Boris bikes are (and how strange that, so long after his change of fortune, we've gone on calling them that). At Mum and Dad's insistence, both of us learnt to drive as soon as we were legally able to, but neither of us had ever owned a car. In London, there's no point, and now I know that I never will.

It was after six when I left work – much later than I'd intended. Afraid that my courage would give out, I pedalled as fast as I could before thinking got in the way. Caught up in the fumes and sheer bad manners of rush-hour traffic, I barely noticed crossing the bridge, but as I subsided into the smaller streets south of the river, the street lighting became more sporadic, and I realised it was dark.

When I got to the house the police tape was gone, and instead of a dilapidated door I was met by a dark interior. The door was ajar and tied to its handle was a bunch of flowers. What on earth? They were purple and white, pretty garden flowers, hand-picked, it seemed, and still quite fresh. A lovely gesture; should have thought of it myself, but who could have put them there? I wanted to know who it was that shared my love for Phil. There was no sign of life in the house.

I couldn't see a bell. The street lights were pathetic – enough to shed an eerie light on the flowers but not strong enough to show me the immediate interior or what lay beyond. I knocked on the door, tentatively called out "hello?" and, heart thumping, put one foot over the threshold. I looked around for some sort of push button that might flood the hall and stairs with the light of normality. But there was none to be seen and, in any case, I sensed that light would only have confirmed the ugliness of what was already visible. I stood still and listened. Nothing. I'm not easily frightened but I was in a shaky state and anyway have always been anxious about trespassing. And that dark emptiness somehow spoke of its witness to horror. Why was the door open? It was an invitation, but an invitation to God knew what.

I shook myself. What was I thinking of, going at night? Come on, get a grip, girl, come back in daylight, and get it in perspective. And I gave in to my body's urge to flee.

* * *

Most of the time I could almost believe that Phil was alive. As I hadn't seen him much recently, I could carry with me the presence of his living self, the boy and man I'd loved. I still hadn't been back to that ghastly place, with those flowers, that smell of death. I was thankful to leave it behind like a bad dream, not a part of the reality of my lovely brother. But I also knew there was something unfinished, and I felt a strong sense of kinship with whoever had cared enough to put the flowers there. Of course he had friends that I didn't know, but I couldn't imagine anyone who would live in a place like that, or put flowers there without saying a word. And not any old flowers either, put together by some florist and anonymised in cellophane, but picked or bought personally, and tied with ribbon. Blood red ribbon.

After a couple of weeks, I couldn't bear it any longer. That house, those flowers, interfered with my working day, as images superimposed on my screen, on the papers I shuffled on my desk. I knew I had to go back, to exorcise those images from my life.

Flowers. Yes, I'd take some, better than the wretchedly impersonal bunch the florist had sent to the funeral. Just a few, nothing showy.

Something personal to mark the spot, carefully chosen, stem by stem, to show that the anonymous donor wasn't the only one who cared. After all, those other flowers would be pretty well dead by now.

I didn't like to think about it but couldn't help wondering why Phil had been there, who he could have been visiting in that sordid place. On my way there, I promised myself that I would go up those stairs and find out once and for all what was there, but when I arrived, the presence of that wretched woman drove everything from my mind.

I cycled home in a desperate fury, leaving my own flowers scattered on the ground. I parked the bike at my local docking station and almost ran round the corner to my flat, breathing fast, and desperate to recapture my usual pleasure at arriving at my own front door. Inside, I tried to recover some sort of normality. Dropping my bag and coat on the settee, I paced around, pulling down the blinds, my fingers itching from those days when lighting up had given me some much-needed relief. As it was, a glass of wine and a bath with some smellies would have to do.

Chapter 12

After that appalling day, Emma kept away – how could she not? – but she was haunted.

For once her routine didn't satisfy. When she got to work, she put out the newspapers and the new issue of *The Journal of Hellenic Studies*. She scanned and copied, sent books off to the binders, and smiled at the Fellows. She went through the motions, but her mind was elsewhere. After work, she walked round the garden with unseeing eyes; she stroked the cats with an absent mind; and listened to Melvyn Bragg with only half an ear, realising when the 10 o'clock pips went that she hadn't really grasped what they were talking about. And when she went to bed, she lay awake. She was restless; she was troubled.

Unlike Denise, who claimed that having children had destroyed her sleep patterns, Emma had always felt rather superior about sleeping soundly; it was only at times of crisis that sleep eluded her, so it was a rare experience to lie awake, listening to the wind in the trees, the click of the cat flap, and the occasional sound of a passing car.

Once the shock of the encounter wore off, Emma's analytical mind kicked in. When she'd first seen the flowers, it had been more a question of what they had stirred in her, than the reality behind them – who they were for. She was caught up in an anguish which for all these years she had so successfully suppressed. Why had it erupted now? She had seen such flowery tributes before. Painful as they were, they had never before had such an impact on her. Was it her "time of life"? Like PMT, truthful, just exaggerated? To abuse her languages horribly: *in menopauso veritas*?!

In the long and empty wastes of sleeplessness, Emma's mind wouldn't stop. She wondered about that girl. She was so striking, with those enviably long legs and that glorious red mane. Was

Emma imagining it, or were her eyes different colours? Where did she come from? Did she live there? It seemed unlikely. Surely, she would have refreshed the flowers before now. And Emma couldn't associate that vibrant girl with a shabby, shady place like that and those dingy stairs. What could it be? Why was the door open? And who went up there?

Emma tried to put the whole thing out of her mind. But images of the dead flowers, the dark doorway and the shouting girl kept bouncing back into her consciousness. Sometimes when she was at the edge of sleep they would rocket back to the forefront of her senses. What was it all about? And, most of all, why did she care?

The nighttime disturbances were extended by a need to get up and change sheets that were drenched by the sweats that assailed her several times a night. She couldn't bear to lie down again on damp and clammy sheets. And in any case, her mother's voice warned her that she could catch her death. She'd had to replace her winceyette nighties that she had found with such trouble – she was a chilly mortal – with thinner ones of pure cotton.

Was there no part of her life unaffected by the Big M? The worst of it was that no one could tell her how long this would all go on. From a few months (really?) to ten years and more, from what she could gather. It had already been with her for more than six months, and showed no signs of abating.

However, no amount of emotional disturbance could disrupt Emma's iron-solid daytime routine. Indeed, it was all the more important now to withstand the eddies of chaos. With an early start, it was good not to have to think. Every night she laid the table for breakfast, and usually made sandwiches to take in for lunch. Though towards the end of the week, when she was running out of food, she sometimes treated herself to something at the little café jutting out over the river near Lambeth Bridge. In the evenings she cooked. She had learned plain cooking at her mother's knee and had no wish to alter her habits. There was no call for a Sunday roast when cooking for one, but otherwise she stuck pretty much to what she'd eaten at home. Her mother, born in the thirties, had lived through the war and rationing, and was used to being careful. Emma saw no reason to depart from the common sense of that practice, whereas Denise had burst out into a way of life that seemed to Emma like extravagance. Goodness knows where she got the money. But for Denise worry was a foreign language, and she'd never cared about debt. Low interest rates had just encouraged her recklessness. "The only good place to be," she was wont to say, "is in the red."

Every night too Emma spread her clothes out on the bedroom chair, together with her shiny pointed shoes. She'd always taken pride in the elegance of her narrow feet. She had three skirts of the same style, all to the mid-calf, with a kick pleat in the back for easy movement especially on the bike, and she alternated them throughout the week, with sweaters in the winter, and blouses for warmer days. All good, serviceable clothes. She didn't remember the last time she had shown her knees. As the old song said, it used to be considered shocking. Shocking, yes. Times changed. When it was warm, she had a couple of long-sleeved dresses. Trousers were not permissible at work. If Emma had minded in the past, any such objections had long since faded from her mind. That was how it was. Trousers were for the weekend and the garden.

The garden was her haven, especially on fine summer evenings, when she could wind down after work, a glass of wine in hand, watching the birds flutter their way to their sleeping places before the sun went down. She tried to ignore the little jobs that always needed doing, and just to relax in the tranquillity of the place.

The garden was a resting place as well as a place of new growth. Tramp, the little stray cat that she'd cared for until he got leukaemia, was buried in one corner, a hedgehog in the other. Not that Emma could have performed the task herself – she was too squeamish. It was the good-natured Denise who had come over to bury them deep, to stop Emma's cats or any roaming fox from digging them up. Emma almost fantasised about joining them, when her time came, squeezed in a little corner of the land that she had nurtured, among the trees and shrubs she'd planted. It was possible, apparently. Denise had once been to the burial of a friend's father in his own garden. Buried under the cherry tree, where he'd loved to sit. Although Emma had originally been shocked by the idea, it actually sounded rather beautiful. But, of course, it wasn't something she would actually do. People like her didn't.

Chapter 13

With my brother's death, my heart had gone out of me. The police were predictably uninformative. They couldn't tell me anything about what happened, or who lived in the house: "I'm sorry, Madam, I really couldn't say." A passerby had found him in the morning, bleeding, on the pavement just outside. Hit and run. One-way street, driving the wrong way, much too fast. No local CCTV. No witnesses. Or none that had had the guts to come forward. The constable made it sound as if it happened all the time. Maybe it did.

About a year before he died, I learnt something about Phil that worried me. Apparently, his ill-paid charity job was only part of his life, a sort of cover for where his passion lay: in a project that went much nearer – dangerously near – to the core of the matter.

As we sometimes did, we met for a drink after work, and he was fidgety, nervous, looking round the bar.

"What's up, Phil?"

"It's just something I'm working on. It worries me."

But he wouldn't tell me what it was, just gave me the address of his blog and said under his breath, "Have a look, Sis. But keep it under your hat, won't you?"

And when I got home, I did have a look, and worried immediately that someone might track what I was looking at – they can do that these days, can't they? Was this legal? More than that, was it safe? I believed in all of this, of course I did. But it was so extreme.

I didn't look again, and tried to forget about it. I didn't want the sort of life where I had to keep looking over my shoulder. My own career choice was unremarkable – there are plenty of civil servants in our family, including Dad. But Phil was different. From an early age we had shared a passion for politics. But while I had seen a clear career path to influencing policy, Phil seemed to have needed another, riskier, way.

He'd always been more radical, and although it wasn't my way, I *had always admired his courage, his ability to stay with uncomfortable truths, whatever the consequences. He'd never said, but I always felt that he found my approach wishy-washy, that he considered I was living a life of compromise. That was all very well, but as a civil servant I have to be careful. For instance, I stay away from social media. I'm on various apps because that's where the conversations happen, but I don't often tweet or otherwise make myself visible. It's odd for someone of our generation, but I'm not prepared to make myself an easy target. It's just not worth risking attracting the attention of some journalist keen to dig up the dirt.*

As it is, I often struggle with government policy, especially now I'm in the Home Office. For most of my career it hasn't actually been a problem because, despite the public rhetoric, there is in fact little policy difference between the parties. In fact, some Tory justice ministers have been more enlightened than the Labour ones and, as we've all learnt now, sometimes ministers from the same party differ more than they do from those of the opposition. Who would have thought, for instance, that the same party would, within a few years, ban books from prisons, then introduce a more educational, resettlement agenda? But with this lot, it's different; the strain on my conscience is greater. I hear from older colleagues that it was much the same when Thatcher came in.

After ten years in the service, I've got used to the fact that my capacity for influencing policy is minimal. The daily routine is becoming a bit of a grind. I still find my work stimulating, but too often it's become a matter of coping with budget cuts and managing the dynamics in the department. Some of the older men still find it hard to be managed by a woman. They don't say so, but it seems pretty clear from the way they behave. Honestly, what century are they living in!

And then we were plunged into mayhem, into what many consider the greatest administrative challenge since the war. Not a single department was unaffected by planning for our exit from Europe. We're used to change, pride ourselves on our ability to adjust, but

Brexit was something else. It didn't help, though I understood the reasons, that we were forbidden to do any contingency planning. I thought I'd worked hard before, but that was as nothing to what was demanded of us now. With all the previous staffing cuts and now poaching to fill the new departments, there simply weren't enough of us to get everything done. And, unsurprisingly, my staff were upset, worried about their jobs. A lot of my time was spent in reassurance.

And all this happened just after my move to the Home Office! No one could say that the last few years have been boring, but it's not exactly how I imagined my time in a new department would be spent.

When I told Phil of my promotion and move, he pulled a face. "Watch your step, Sis," was all he said, and I didn't ask him to explain. I guess I didn't want to hear.

Soon after our conversation, he disappeared. No one knew where he was but I wasn't all that worried – he was bad about keeping in touch at the best of times, and I knew he'd pop up again, as he always did.

But this time he didn't. The first I heard of him was the announcement of his death. And so began the nightmare. The searing pain, and then the questions. Questions from the police, who were kind enough, but persistent:

"What was your brother doing at the house? Where had he been?"

To which my answer could only be: "I'm sorry, I don't know, I have no idea." No doubt Mum and Dad had been subjected to the same questions with the same result. They would know even less than me. In fact, I couldn't think of anyone who would have any idea of what Phil had been up to.

But, more painfully, there were the interminable questions in my own mind, over and over again. Why? How? And the worm of doubt: was it just an accident, or something else?

And then, of course, someone had to identify his body. I couldn't expect Mum and Dad to. They were in pieces. So I did it. The police were kind, drove me there and said, "Take your time," but nothing can prepare you for such a terrible thing. As I looked down at the dear pale face above the sheet, it was the first time I'd seen my brother for about a year. With tears running down my cheeks, I murmured in my heart, "Oh my darling Phil, what have they done to you? Where have you been?"

* * *

I was in a terrible state. Bursting into tears at the drop of a hat. Even after compassionate leave, it was all I could do to keep up appearances at work. Everyone was very kind, but there was a big hole in my sense of self. I wanted to find out more. Wanted to make it up to him, make up for paying so little attention while he was alive. And something was shifting in my own attitudes, especially to work. I found I was less tolerant of political fudging, more questioning of my own commitment to justice. I couldn't help thinking his death had something to do with his project, something "they" didn't want people to know.

A few days later an older, fatherly constable told me a little more. "Well, Miss, it looked as if he'd just come down those stairs. He was, like, half in, half out. The pavement is really narrow there, but the driver had to be out of his skull to go that far off the road."

Chapter 14

The funeral was lavish, held at the church near Mum and Dad's Warwickshire farm. Lavish – and completely inappropriate. The vicar, who hadn't seen Phil since he was about twelve, talked about him as if he had remained the same small boy of his memory. He made a passing reference to Phil's charity work, intimating that he had gone on to greater things in London. The coffin was of the heaviest oak, the furniture of solid brass, as if to make up for what I knew my parents considered a not only short but inadequate life. Phil would have hated it. But afterwards, as I sat at the table with my parents, gaunt and upright in their grief, I knew that this was the only way they had of dealing with Phil's death. It wasn't in my heart to blame them. With dark glasses masking my own red eyes, I was also struggling to cope.

The hotel ballroom was packed. Phil had been popular, and his life had touched people from many different communities and different generations. There was a spread of ages among the mourners. I was surprised how few of them I'd met, and felt again the sadness of realising how little of Phil's life I'd known. There were, of course, some of my parents' friends – mostly the county set, with whom neither I nor Phil had had anything in common, but whom I knew I would be expected to acknowledge. Two couples, tall and patrician, were standing together and, as I approached, were talking about their servants.

"She's very thorough, but I can hardly understand a word she says."

"Yes, now that they're here, you'd think they'd take the trouble to learn the language."

I put on my public smile and received the condolences of people who knew nothing about the adult Philip, and wouldn't have liked him if they had.

I was drawn to the groups of younger people, but there were few that I knew. I spotted Phil's former girlfriend, Rachel, on the other side of the room, but they'd split up a couple of years ago, so she was *unlikely to know anything. I hadn't heard of anyone in Phil's life since then, though, given his habitual taciturnity about his personal life, that didn't mean there hadn't been one. Most of the people there, I imagined, were Phil's former colleagues. I knew little of his work; he'd always played his cards close to his chest. It was hard to break into any of the tightly knit groups, but when I caught sight of one of Phil's former school friends, I made my way towards him. Although Tom was a good deal younger, I'd seen a bit of him when Phil had brought friends home. He was about a foot taller than when I'd last seen him, but there was no mistaking that high forehead and thick-browed brown eyes.*

He was talking to two older people, who turned out to be his parents; his father was very deaf, which in the hubbub of the room made conversation difficult. Eventually I managed to get Tom on his own.

"It's good to see you, Tom. What are you up to these days?" And then, without giving him time to reply, asked the only question that mattered, "Did you see much of Phil?"

"No, not much, actually, not since he moved. And, to tell the truth, we really moved in different worlds. What he did was beyond me, really. He was a good man."

"Yes." My eyes welled up. "Did you…?" I cleared my throat, "Did you have any idea of what he'd been up to recently?"

"Sorry, no. As I said, it must have been a year or more since we spoke. Kept meaning to meet up. You know how it is." He smiled vaguely, and raised his eyes, apparently catching sight of someone across the room. "Oh, excuse me. I must…"

"Of course."

I sipped my wine, wondering when it would be possible to escape. As I pushed my way towards my parents, a hand touched my arm.

"Excuse me. Are you Nicola?"

"Yes?"

He was a thin bearded man, with ill-fitting clothes that might have been borrowed for the occasion.

"I'm Martin." He obviously expected a reply. "He didn't tell you about me?"

"No, sorry. We haven't, hadn't, spoken for a while." I didn't know what to say. "Were you...?"

Martin smiled. "Oh, no, not that. He wasn't gay."

"Oh." I was relieved that there wasn't something else I hadn't known.

"No," said Martin. "He saved my sister's life."

I stared at him. "Heavens. Goodness. Can we...?" And I looked around for a space in which to talk.

"No, not now. I may not stay. We can meet somewhere. I ring you?" I tore a page out of my notebook and scribbled down my number. Martin stuffed the bit of paper in his pocket, and almost ran from the room.

I turned slowly back into the room, wondering what on earth all that had been about. I was pretty sure I wouldn't like what he had to tell me; it was obviously to do with what I'd seen on Phil's blog, not that I could remember it that well. I wished I'd looked at it properly. GRUK, or something – I remembered the "R" stood for "rescue". I worried, as ever, about being compromised, but I had to know. Come what may, I would speak to this man. I would meet him and find out what he had to say.

Chapter 15

It was hard to remember. Emma had nothing of the time when her world had expanded, when her joy had encompassed the vastness of her known world. She had nothing of Johnny's. They had rarely needed to write to each other. In general Johnny's trips were short: "It's not worth my sending a card, darling. I'll be back before it arrives." So he had usually phoned instead. Except that one time at the end, for that longer trip to Prague. And she had that card, treasured, and dog-eared from so many months under her pillow.

My dearest little Emma,

So looking forward to the weekend, and seeing you. Prague is lovely, but I miss you. Maybe we can come here together one day.

All yours,

Johnny

Prague – how she dreamed of such a place. It seemed too good to be true.

Emma knew that Johnny would need some space when he got back from his trip, so it wasn't until the following morning that she became uneasy. The flight had been on time – she had rung to check. At work the following day, Emma kept checking her phone for messages. She made all sorts of excuses for him – tiredness, work preoccupations – but by the evening she was convinced that he had left her, that he wasn't coming back. His phone seemed permanently on voicemail. There was no reaching him.

The weekend came without him, for by that time he was dead, struck down by a lorry on his way back from the airport. No one had thought to let her know. The first she heard was two weeks later when his sister, Dorothy, found her name in Johnny's address book. There had been no public funeral, Dorothy told her, just a small family-only service, and the death was never reported. One road death more or less was of no consequence to any except those most intimately concerned.

Emma was overcome with loss. Of him, to the world and to herself. Of the part of herself that only he had understood. Her sense of self that had flourished under his loving care. The tide of loss covered over all those bright new beginnings. Everything. Sleep eluded her; eating was almost beyond her. There was no question of compassionate leave this time; her relationship was unrecognised by the outside world, so she had to struggle into work. She kept going only because her habitual patterns of living – the conveyor belt from home to work and back – were so ingrained. She shrank, her clothes hung loose. Colleagues looked at her with concern and enquired about her health.

One of the Fellows accosted her in the corridor. "You all right, my dear? You look a little peaky."

"Thank you. Just a little tired, perhaps." Tired of living.

Emma found that she was grieving for two. The loss of her mother, no more than two years before, had been submerged in the busyness of form filling and home-hunting. Barely acknowledged at the time, it now surged up into consciousness. As did anger. How dared they leave her? Why did anyone who was anyone in her life disappear? Starting, of course, with her father.

Johnny's brother and sister were very kind, but she hadn't been with him long enough to be part of any family process. Only the two of them had known how important they had been to each other. Only the postcard, arriving a week later proved that he'd even gone away, that it hadn't been some sort of excuse. So she was alone in her grief except for Denise and Julian, who had been a godsend. With them she didn't have to pretend; there she could sit with emptiness in her eyes and soul and, despite Denise's tendency to jolly her along, on the whole they left her alone. But their open physicality was a painful reminder.

Emma knew that this was not just the end of a chapter. It was more like an amputation. And, like an amputation, the feeling continued. She had been sexually awakened, and simply didn't know what to do with it. Any hope that touch starvation would cower her body into submission was soon dispelled. Her nervous energy increased and yearned for release – and only her own hands could do it.

And she had to get used to being alone again. Until her mother died, she'd never lived alone. And although she had never before had anyone in her life, it felt now as though she always had. Anyway, before that there had been her mother, a steady presence in her life.

Her anger was hard to cope with. To have waited all this time for the love of her life, to have him taken away. Bloody cars. No wonder she'd never wanted to drive. Far too dangerous. She hated to acknowledge it, but maybe Denise and Julian were right in their campaign against the motor car.

In time, work became her salvation. Work and habit. Sucked in first from her mother's milk, and then from her studies of the ancients, was the fundamental importance of effort and perseverance and it had stood her in good stead. It was as if that shiny self had never been. No one would have her now. Why had she imagined otherwise? This was the reality of her life.

Eventually, some comfort emerged in the shape of a postcard pinned to the staff notice-board at work.

Unexpected litter of kittens.

Homes needed,

Pretty, various shades of tabby.

Sweet-natured.

As a family they'd never had dogs or cats. Emma couldn't be doing with canine soppiness, but had always enjoyed the independence of cats, and their lithe silkiness. So she took the plunge and went to have a look. When she saw the kittens, her heart was won and, unknown quantity or not, the two sisters (don't get toms, smelly things) came home with her in a borrowed basket.

But, goodness, how complicated it all was! Basket, food, inoculations, cat litter, collars, magnetic cat door to keep intruders out. But Pinky and Perky were adorable, and soon became a family that she couldn't do without.

Chapter 16

April was not the cruellest month. For Emma, it was November. Even as a child, the darkening days and gloomy weather had depressed her, and she felt no differently now. With nothing but the prospect of ever shortening winter days, there was little to recommend it.

It all started with Halloween. The shops were full of images of skulls and skeletons, and even the London streets, as she made her way home, were dotted with excited young children dressed up in their ghoulish best, preparing to pester their neighbours. How coarse the masks were, compared with those of the ancient Greeks, which were simple, powerful and effective.

Not that Emma was tricked or treated at home. In her little community the children were too young to be troublesome, except Sandra, who was too sensible and too busy, and anyway, her mother would never have let her go door-knocking on her own. But in the office Marilyn was full of stories of how she had either to appease the streams of children who came to the door in sinister disguises, or hide under the bedclothes, pretending to be out. And since Mexico's Day of the Dead had been brought to public attention, the whole macabre business seemed to linger on into early November. Emma knew the festival was supposed to be celebratory. But she didn't live in a culture that celebrated the dead. When someone died, it was seen as the end. Full stop. Move on.

And then came Remembrance Day itself. "Lest we forget". It was hardly likely when reminders were everywhere. Services on the nearest Sunday to the anniversary, then on 11 November itself. It was a day that reminded Emma of her grandfather, who always watched the service at the Cenotaph on the news: a time when he went into himself, remembering the friends that he had survived. Poor old thing: she wished she'd known him longer, when she was a proper adult, and could have conversed with him on equal terms.

On 19 November, wearing black and holding her umbrella in front of her face, Emma walked along Piccadilly to the church. She wasn't wearing a poppy. She had bought one as usual, but as usual had discarded it immediately after the eleventh. It seemed so sad that such a pretty, delicate little flower should be associated with the slaughter of millions. And she hardly needed a reminder. The date for the RoadPeace service for traffic victims was always fixed in her mind; on the third Sunday it was conveniently soon after Remembrance Day. The one blended into the other. Pointless deaths, one way or another.

Emma had been to the service once before, immediately after Johnny's death. She'd heard something on the radio, and had clung to anything that might help but, when it came to it, she'd been far too shy, too traumatised, to talk to anyone. Goodness knew why she was going now, after all this time. But she found it comforting. It was religious, and she wasn't, but she found the prayers affecting as they were designed to be. And she liked the fact that there were talks by people of different faiths. It made the scale of it more evident, really. It wasn't just a local thing, it was worldwide, and there were any number of services. This year, as before, Emma sat in the church, her throat tight, mouthing the words familiar to her from school, but thinking only of Johnny. She stood for the hymns, but found it hard to sing.

Then, as people gathered in groups afterwards, she was arrested by the sight of – could it be? Yes, the girl of the flowers, the girl on the Boris bike, though her hair was now smoothed back from her face. She did have extraordinary eyes: they were of slightly different colours – one, as she had thought, with a tinge of green. Emma was at the same time terrified and drawn to speak to her. Come on, what can she do to you? But as she tentatively made her way towards her, it was the girl who fled.

Wove her way out of the church, into the street. She disappeared. Emma had no idea who she was or where to find her.

It was dark when Emma left the church, and still raining. At home she barely glanced at the garden on her nightly feeding of the compost, trudging down the path in her wellies and the wet, her eyes only on her feet. All around her was the sodden decay of summer's flowering and, although she knew the ground was still soft enough to allow her to move some plants, maybe put in some bulbs, she just didn't have the heart to think about it. She was below par – not ill enough to take any time off, just lacking the energy or willpower to do anything much. In any case, with no one to replace her, it was hard to take time off, and she wouldn't have dreamt of pretending, asking for what Marilyn called "gardening leave". She was shocked at the very idea. Anyway, Emma didn't get ill. She didn't really believe in illness, except as a failure of a well regimented life – she was in that, at least, her mother's child.

That evening she was at a loose end. Sometimes the reality of living alone came home to her. She was tired of having to initiate everything, provide her own stimulus, especially in cold weather when the garden held few attractions. Tired of having to sort everything, from the drains to the stove. She was tired of being so damn *responsible.* And at work, everything was down to her. The trustees were supportive, but only she could run the library and do everything that needed to be done. Of course she valued her independence, but sometimes it was just all too much. Her job, her house, even the cats. She longed to have some fun, whatever that might mean. She found it hard to imagine doing anything just to please herself. Usually, she was tired enough after work, cooking supper and clearing up but tonight she was wide awake. The cats were out, there was nothing on the television and it was too early to go to bed. Emma wandered aimlessly around the house and wondered what to do. What she needed was a bit of tender loving care. That's what Johnny used to say. "What you could do with, my Em," he would say, "is a bit of TLC."

The following morning, Emma was a little sluggish, woken by the alarm and wishing for once that she could spend a couple of hours longer in bed. But as she rode to the station, the cold brightness of the day cheered her, and a pat on the back from the trustees over her cataloguing of the archives lent a sunnier glow to her mood. It had been an arduous task, and she welcomed the recognition. In the evening, with a jacket round her shoulders, she stood at her back doorway, leaning against the frame, gazing at the trees, leafless now, but standing proud against the clarity of the night sky. The cats were skittish, scrambling up trees, chasing each other and their tails. For however short a time, it was important to remember that life could be good.

* * *

As the days passed, the rhythm and demands of work took over and I began to breathe. We were interviewing for a new manager, and it was pretty time-consuming. It didn't help that training budgets had been cut so there was little to offer someone coming from outside. I felt as if I were living parallel lives. Amid the fraught busyness of my work days there was one thing I was determined to do. I'd been googling like mad to try to find anything that would help me cope, would make me feel that I wasn't going crazy, find other people who felt like this. Among all the awful stories of death, bereavement, anguish and bodies under cars I clutched at the fact that every year there was a service for people who have lost friends and family on the roads, people like me. And it was just coming up.

It was such an effort to make myself go – such a scary thing to do. All day I worried that I wouldn't make it, that I would break down, but I forced myself to walk up Piccadilly up to the entrance of St James's, and through the door of the church. Although I'm not a churchy person, the service did help, as did knowing there were others there who were suffering as I was. But when the service was over, unbelievably I saw, sitting sedately near the front, that wretched woman again. Why did I run away? I regretted it almost immediately. What was it about her that spooked me so? It felt as if she was stalking me but she couldn't have known I'd be there.

Chapter 17

Winter came and Emma's world closed in. During the dark months that followed, it was hard to be optimistic, hard to believe that the shoots of spring would ever break through the unresponsive earth. She gave little thought to the door, the flowers, or the girl, and, when thoughts arose, she stamped on them. She was travelling to work by bus so there were no visual reminders. She told herself that she was content to spend her days in the womb of the library and at night to hurry home to her wood stove, the cats and her hot water bottle. And on Friday nights to greet the weekend's leisure with her evening at Bob's.

* * *

When Charlie was about six weeks old, Marilyn brought him into the office to show him off. With a bag hanging from either hand, and the baby in a sling plastered to her front, she swept into the staffroom to a warm welcome from the rest of the staff, who gathered round to coo.

Emma had missed Marilyn's cheerful presence and had wondered how she was getting on. When a card arrived at the office announcing the birth, Emma had sent some flowers, and had been invited to visit, but Croydon was a bit far, and it didn't feel quite appropriate, really. They weren't that close.

Emma had never before witnessed the gestation of a baby, and was curious to see what had emerged. Having seen Charlie expand his mother's belly from week to week, it was quite something to see the living result. Astonishing, really. And he was delightful. A cherubic chubbiness; an enchanting little face with a pair of long-lashed blue eyes peeping out from the safety of his sling. Emma was touched by Marilyn's protective warmth. She had no doubt that she would prove a loving mother: it would be a natural extension of her generous friendly nature. She seemed born for giving. Seeing them together, Emma felt that Charlie's arrival was a joyfully accepted reward. How lovely it must be to be so close.

"Ah," said short-sighted Trevor, craning forward to look, "what an enchanting smile."

"Wind," said the fond mother.

Marilyn's size, strangely, didn't seem to have reduced much since they'd last seen her. Her belly was smaller, of course, but her bust was if anything larger. But she did look different: her face was thinner, she looked older, more settled somehow. No longer a girl.

Denise had of course gone through the same process, but Emma had seen little of it. She'd only seen her sister once or twice during her pregnancy and then, all of a sudden, there had been darling little Posy. Her niece. And Denise too had settled, calmed down, and then met her Julian. Happy ever after, it was to be hoped.

Being a largely male establishment, the club had little provision for women. The ladies consisted of only two cubicles, and a small hand-washing area, in which Marilyn was ensconced, one mountainous breast exposed, calmly feeding Charlie. Emma had never seen such a thing: the breast was monstrous, bigger than the baby's head, so unlike her own little buttons. She had, of course, seen Denise naked when they were growing up, but when her mother was dying, she had guarded her modesty from her daughter, bringing in a carer for the more intimate tasks. So Emma had barely seen her mother's body except in the last days, when occasionally, the nightdress would slip away, revealing her hardly visible breasts, sinking into the bones of her ribs as she lay on her back: barely raised saucers, centred by a pale aureole. Emma had not wanted to look but was caught somehow by their piteous beauty. She had certainly never been faced with what faced her now: the frank nudity of a single breast prised in all its ripeness out of the neckline of a top. Despite her liberal pretensions, Emma was shocked. She really didn't want to see it. Nature was sometimes quite hard to take.

When she saw Emma, Marilyn looked up and laughed. "Little glutton, can't get enough. Thought I'd better feed him in here. Didn't want to shock the old dears." Emma dived into one of the cubicles and tried to recover her composure.

Chapter 18

For some months, Emma had felt Christmas looming. It wasn't the glitter in the shops – she tended to avoid them – nor the ads for presents on television. It was the emotional countdown. By the time it came, she was exhausted. Strange, she thought, how when a holiday came along, it seemed impossible to do another thing, although she knew that if it had been a week later, or earlier for that matter, the same would have been true. The energy stretched just to where it had to, and no further.

Emma had mixed feelings about the festival. It was always good to have time off, and on the whole, she liked going down to stay with Denise and Julian – especially if Posy was there. They were always good to her, and it was a relief not to have to think about shopping and cooking for a few days. She didn't even mind vegetarian food, though she was always pleased to go back to her usual diet when she went home. In fact, it had become customary for her to cook Bob a Christmas meal when she returned: a turkey breast, some ham and sausages for the two of them. It wouldn't be Christmas if she didn't have the traditional fare at some point in the holiday. And it was a nice change to have someone to cook for: someone appreciative, unlike her mother who in the latter stages of her life had had no interest in what was put in front of her.

But Denise and the others always made Christmas very festive, with a tree, decorations, mince pies – even crackers. Emma's own contribution was a cake which, like her mother, she always started in November and punctiliously fed with brandy once a week. Denise wouldn't have had the patience.

Julian carried her case upstairs, and Emma followed him. She looked with pleasure round the familiar little attic room, then after a quick wash took out the cake and the presents she had brought, to put round the tree, as tradition dictated – a running shirt for Julian, some new pastels for Denise and, with Marilyn's guidance, some toiletries for Posy. There was a long-standing agreement that no one should spend more than £20.

As she came down the stairs, Denise was putting the finishing touches to the tree.

Emma paused. "Looks nice, Denise. You always do a good job."

"Thanks, well, it's something I enjoy, as you know."

"When's Posy arriving?"

"She's not."

Emma stared at her. "What? Why ever not?"

Squatting with her back to her sister, Denise said shortly, "We fell out."

"Really? Why?" She knew they didn't always see eye to eye, but what could be so serious as to keep them apart at Christmas? "What about?"

"I don't want to talk about it." And then, swivelling round and catching sight of the presents in Emma's hands, said, "And she doesn't want any presents. Says it's hypocritical."

"But what's she going to do for Christmas?"

"Friends, apparently." Denise sniffed. "Just as well. We'd only have rowed." She stood and stretched her back.

Emma looked sadly at the carefully wrapped presents, bought with such care, and the little gluten-free cake for her niece that she had been at such pains to make. So much for that. She wouldn't have bothered, if she'd known: she herself didn't believe in allergies but was too polite to say so. She'd just have to take it back with her. She felt an unreasonable resentment at Posy's absence. For the past six months, Posy had been living in a flat-share in New Cross, but Emma hadn't seen as much of her as she'd hoped. They'd met once for lunch, but Posy had been a bit rushed and had said nothing of her plans. In any case, they were neither of them given to confidences. Emma had thought they might travel down together. She'd left a message on Posy's phone, but there had been no response. Emma didn't like to persist: calling mobiles was so expensive.

"Actually" – Denise couldn't keep it in – "she's going to join the police."

"The *police*?"

"Yes, imagine. My daughter."

Emma didn't know what to say. Rebellion took strange turns. Weakly, she said, "I'm sorry you've fallen out."

Sharply: "Well, you couldn't expect me to approve."

"No." Indeed. "I suppose not."

Hands on hips, Denise confronted her sister. "Honestly, Em, why would she? All that right-wing shit. We'll probably find ourselves facing each other at some demo. Imagine being arrested by your own daughter!"

As Emma tried to picture it, Denise continued. "On her feet all day, in those boots, and a *uniform*!" Then, more urgently, "And I can't help worrying, Em. Will she be safe?"

"Being in the police might be tricky with that name," Emma thought, and to her horror found she had spoken her thought.

Denise stared at her. "What's that supposed to mean?"

"Well..." Oh dear.

"I'm the one who was landed with a ghastly name. Denise! What kind of name is that?"

"Well, you could always have changed it." Trying to lighten the mood, Emma said with a little laugh, "Be grateful that Mum found religion after we were born. Just imagine what names we might have been saddled with!"

Denise glared. "Trust you to take Posy's side. You always have."

Emma was at a loss. "I don't... I don't know what you mean."

Denise ran her hands through her hair. "I could do without all this. I'm stressed enough as it is."

"Are you? I'm sorry, I didn't realise. What about?"

"Work, mostly."

Emma showed her surprise. "But I thought you really liked it."

"I do. But there's not much of it, is there? With all these cuts, it's getting harder to get sessional work. It would be good to be recognised for what I do. Especially for the painting – that's really what I want to spend my time on, instead of chasing any job application that looks remotely possible." Denise subsided on to the settee and examined her nails.

"Surely, Denise, it's what you wanted?" Denise had never wanted a "job". She'd always said that what she wanted was the freedom to express herself. If the price she paid for that was insecurity, then so be it. Better, she always said, than being tied to a job she disliked. There weren't that many choices open to her, but they were ones she would have made anyway.

"What choices do you think I had? Sure, I wouldn't have wanted to sit at a desk all day; that would have killed me, but do you realise how much of a struggle it is, just to keep going? Making enough to live on? And keeping believing in myself?"

"I'm sorry. I had no idea." Emma spoke formally but her heart, if not expressed, was touched. You're so young, is what she wanted to say. Her strong and cheerful sister, who had always seemed invincible, sailing through life without a care.

Denise turned to her an accusing face: "No, you didn't, did you? You always imagine my life is plain sailing. Doesn't it ever occur to you how *exhausting* it is always being cheerful? All that time when Mummy was ill, coming in and cheering you both up, because you were living with her, and then going home and bawling my eyes out."

Emma couldn't speak. How dare she! *And how do you think it felt always taking responsibility, always being there, always trying to cope, instead of swanning in every now and then to be greeted like the Prodigal Son?* All this she said in her head and heart, but not aloud. She never did. She thought back to that time, of her loneliness, of the endless chores for an unbearably

94

uncomplaining mother, of the paperwork, the endless phone calls to doctor and nurse, fielding calls from concerned friends whom her mother didn't want to see, the resentment at being expected to carry it all.

And yet. An uncomfortable little voice reminded her of her relief at opening the door to the smiling face of her sister, of finding some respite from her own pain and the suffering in front of her. Denise had been a fresh breeze from another world. It was true – and she had thought her sister callous at the time – yes, there had been an inkling of that.

Denise brushed her hair from her face, and puffed out a breath. "Oh, don't mind me. I'm just tired. I'll get over it. Come on, you must be hungry. I think we can eat."

But Emma did mind. The meal felt blighted by not only Posy's absence, but by Denise's unaccustomed sharpness. She'd thought her own state was precarious enough. What on earth was going on with them both? Her first selfish thought was "Thank God for Julian," that she would not again be called upon to be the first point of call.

Supper was an uncomfortable affair, with Julian making light conversation in the face of long silences from the other two. Emma wanted an early night, but was persuaded to stay and watch the news with the others. It wasn't something she ever did at home. The "news" was always so depressing, not something she wanted ringing in her ears before bedtime. It was Channel 4, of course, the only one they trusted, but even so Denise and Julian argued with the speakers – their normal way of watching TV. There was a special feature on undercover police – the strain, and excitement, of living a lie.

"And who pays for them?" clamoured Denise. "And what about the women they duped? Oh yes, there was an apology some years ago, but it still goes on, doesn't it? All those ruined lives." Of course Denise was right, though Emma wouldn't have put it so strongly. Deception supposedly "in the public service":

what an appalling way to live your life.

Denise was in full swing: " Imagine living with those lies. All those children with fathers who disappeared." Turning to her sister: "Just like us, eh, Em? Who knows? Perhaps Dad was one of them."

Emma bristled. "Denise, don't be ridiculous. What could you know about it? You were only a baby."

Denise pulled a face. " Just sayin'. Come on, Em, don't take everything so seriously. Of course I've no idea. Just an amusing thought."

Amusing? Really?

In her attic room, Emma lay on her back, gazing sightlessly at the dark ceiling. Goodness, Denise was in troublesome mode tonight. Her earlier comments bounced back into Emma's mind. Was she the sort of person that demanded cheerfulness? A worm of doubt wriggled its way to the surface, and she felt the edge of her security crumbling. Had this been true of her lighthearted Johnny too?

Unsurprisingly, she barely slept. She sweated, she cooled; she threw the duvet off, then pulled it on. Her inability to change her nightie and sheets made her wish for the familiar comforts of home.

* * *

Christmas dawned bright and sharply frosty. Emma woke at her usual time and lay in bed in the dark. There was definitely something missing. Christmas morning wasn't the same without the smell of a turkey that had been cooking all night. There was nothing for her to do, so she decided to stay snug until the rest of the household stirred. The Aga in the kitchen was wonderfully warm, but it was a long way from her unheated bedroom, and she didn't fancy the journey. Not for the first time, the thought crossed her mind that Denise's green credentials were bought at the cost of the comfort of their guests.

She was tired but calmer as she reflected on the exchanges of the previous evening. Did Denise really think that about their father? She wished she knew her sister better. They had never talked properly since childhood; had always lived in different worlds. They probably voted for different parties. Emma had never asked, for fear of being snubbed.

Even when little, Denise had always played up and Emma remembered feeling both cross and scared that her sister would get them both into trouble. As the elder, Emma tended to get the blame, but she was a good girl. She had never sought trouble. Denise had been naughty enough for two. While they were growing up, Emma envied Denise the lightness with which she lived in the world. She envied her apparently untroubled soul. Emma couldn't help feeling that it would be lovely to be so relaxed. But she couldn't imagine it. Oh yes, Denise cared passionately about all sorts of causes, but her life didn't seem hard going, in the way it always had for Emma.

But when she found her métier, Emma had also found her equilibrium. As Denise flitted from one temporary job to another, getting a bit of work here and there, Emma had bedded in at the club. She had found her niche, her security. She had her domain.

On this Christmas morning, she got up eventually, unwilling to face the new day. No one bothered much with breakfast – there was too much to do – and Emma, not wanting to get in the way, made do with a cup of tea and an apple, which she took to the sitting room, and sat on the window seat, gazing out at the dull winter scene. Although she was happy to help, she sensed that the couple would rather have the kitchen to themselves. She could hear some giggling from the kitchen. Without Posy there was no distraction from the love birds. Emma felt the discomfort of her gooseberry status, and longed to be on her own.

Faced with a meal she wouldn't have chosen and didn't

want, Emma tackled the celeriac and cheese pie with untypical truculence. After lunch Julian tactfully busied himself with the dishes, and Denise, her face flushed by wine, the heat of the Aga and a morning's cooking, flung herself down in an armchair opposite her sister. Irritated by Emma's sulkiness, Denise burst out: "What on earth's the matter with you? This isn't like you."

"I'm not like me. I feel quite peculiar. I don't know what's going on. I suppose it's my time of life."

Denise laughed. "Oh, is that all!"

Stung, Emma cried out: "No, it's not all. By the end of next year, I might be out of a job."

"Really? Oh..." Knowing how much her job meant to her, Denise for once bit her tongue. "I'm sorry. What happened?"

"At the last staff review they hinted – well, more than hinted – that it was time I retired."

"But you're nowhere near retirement age."

"No, but there's a tradition that people go at 55. And, besides," Emma hesitated before confiding her greatest fear. Speaking it would make it concrete. "I might not be able to do the job anyway. I might..."she turned her head away, "I might... be going blind."

"What?"

"I've got macular degeneration, the dry sort. There's no cure."

Her sister's kindness was almost unbearable. It nearly broke her heart. Not since Johnny died had Denise been so kind. And, with tears streaming down her face, Emma allowed her sister to hold her, leaning into the embrace with all the need born of years of loneliness.

On Boxing Day, Emma sat on her bed, fully clothed, case packed, waiting for the departure time. Denise would, she knew, appear ten minutes before they needed to leave. Emma knew there was no point in flapping, but she liked to be ready. Denise was the dearest person in all the world, the only person who Emma felt knew her at all, but they couldn't have been more different. With her sister she felt more alive, but was also irritated by the difference between them that felt sometimes like a criticism of self. And she was always glad to come back to the casual indifference of her cats and the habitual rhythms of her solitude.

The returning coach couldn't go fast enough. Emma sat in the mid-afternoon darkness, staring out of the smeary window and willing the miles away. Despite Denise's real concern, Emma kept returning to the way her sister had shouted at her the previous night. A sharp arrow of accusation, the expression of a resentment that had been brewing – on both sides – for all these years. So much for a time of respite and family celebration. Emma returned to her little house like a homing pigeon, thinking of nothing but being in a safe, familiar place. Despite a sense of relief, she was still in a shaky state and she entered into the arrangements for cooking for Bob with little of her usual enthusiasm.

As it happened, the evening had to be delayed until early January. Bob had suffered "a little turn", as he put it, and needed to rest up until he was fit enough to entertain. In her house next door, Emma couldn't settle. She was restless at night and full of foreboding during the day. The row had upset her. She had always avoided confrontation, usually successfully. It was Denise and her mother who had rowed, Emma who ran to her bedroom and stuck her fingers in her ears.

But it was more than the unexpected row with Denise that had unsettled Emma. There were just a few days before she was due back at work. With worries about her sight and her job, this was not a new year to look forward to. And she didn't know how to cope with the turbulence of this disobedient body. The night before her return to work, she woke at 4 a.m. and, heart thudding, sat bolt upright in bed, the image of that TV programme before her eyes.

What if that was it? Not her father at all, but Johnny. What if he had never died? Just disappeared like the police in the programme? What if his love – which had always seemed too good to be true – had been a sham? And then her reasoning mind kicked in. What would he have had to gain from it? She was no activist. But some of those cops filled in their cover stories by linking up with completely innocent women, just to give themselves credibility. All the doubts suppressed over years crawled out on to the surface of her mind: Johnny's unexplained trips abroad, the fact she'd never met his family, that they knew nothing of her. That she'd never really known what happened. Maybe the family were in on it. But, no, they didn't have to phone her. Of course she would never know, she had no way of contacting them, after all these years. Emma told herself to stop chasing shadows: she was being ridiculous; there was no reason to think things were other than they'd seemed. This was just middle-of-the-night paranoia.

Emma forced herself to lie down and cover herself up, then curled into a ball. As she tossed on the now rumpled bed, she tried to think of other things, to count sheep (why sheep?) and to listen to the wind in the trees.

And to her breath, her rather ragged breath. She'd never been much aware of her breath except when she was short of it, when she'd been running for a bus or cycling uphill. Focusing on breath was something Denise went on about. It was all very well for those with time on their hands, but in a busy life like Emma's there was too much else to think about. Breath just happened.

But now she turned on her back and, as a distraction more than anything, she listened to her breathing: big breath in – stuttering breath out – in – out. Amazing, really: a rhythm of life. In – out, in – longer breath out, And so, as Emma consciously smoothed her breath, she finally soothed herself into sleep.

Chapter 19

When morning came, Emma found that she was right: night fears had retreated, reason was re-established, and she found that after all it was good to get back into her usual routine; good to see the smiling faces of her colleagues, and to share the usual holiday experiences. Even so, she felt a little distanced. Trevor had finally retired; there was no Marilyn; and Emma felt a pang when she heard of the death of Dr Plummer a week or so before. He'd been in his nineties, true, but had been the most faithful of the Fellows, having arrived at the library every day for as long as anyone could remember, so his corner seat was not only empty but poignant.

That's what men did. They died. Or disappeared. Or, rather, her rational mind admonished, hers did. Not everyone's. Julian looked as if he was staying around. Denise seemed to have found a good one this time, one that was in for the long haul. And Marilyn's partner, Nick, seemed decent enough. Emma had seen him once, when he'd left work early to collect Marilyn for a weekend away. He was a handsome full-faced man with a shock of dark hair, a bank clerk now, apparently – was that what they were called these days? He worked in a bank, anyway.

On the bus back to the station that night, Emma couldn't help thinking of what she might have been seeing if she'd been on her bike. She shook herself. She had things other than a dark interior and flowers on her mind; she had to prepare for the post-Christmas meal with Bob.

* * *

As Emma stood on his doorstep the following Saturday, with bags of goodies at her feet, Bob welcomed her with his usual warmth: "My dear, how lovely. Do come in. How are you? How was Christmas?"

"Better not to ask."

"Ah, like that, eh? Families! Still, here we are. It's good to see you."

And Emma unwound as she served the meal, carefully cooked in her own oven, and transported the few yards to his house. They ate the turkey and trimmings in harmony, leaving the pudding, by mutual consent, to a little later in the day. Emma washed up then they relaxed in front of the fire. Conversation swayed this way and that with the ease of old friends.

"And another thing," said Bob, as he sipped the last of his wine, "I don't want to be resuscitated."

Emma stared. "What on earth makes you think of that, you silly thing? You're quite recovered now."

"I mean when the time comes. That last bout made me think. It's time I got myself sorted. I've made an appointment with old Bernard to do my Will."

"Yes, I suppose that's a good idea, I ought to re-do mine, I suppose." Though she couldn't think how her life had changed since she'd last done it. Life didn't change.

"So, I hope you'll witness it. I'll get Dave from the garage to be the other witness. Oh, and Emma," he turned to her, "I need to think about how I want my funeral to be."

Emma banged down her glass. "Oh, for God's sake, Bob!"

The old man's eyes widened. "Emma? What on earth's the matter?"

Emma unclenched her fists and drew breath. "Sorry. Sorry, Bob. I didn't mean... It's just... There's been enough death lately. It's getting on top of me."

"I'm sorry, my dear, I didn't know." Bob was too discreet to pry, but reached out to squeeze her hand.

The afternoon didn't recover, and Emma left early, pleading a headache. The old man leant out of his front door, calling after her: "But, Emma, your pudding!"

As she let herself in to her own front door Emma wondered at herself. In truth what was there for Bob to know? She didn't know, either, why she burst out like that, except that these days her emotions were barely under her control. There was no excuse, no recent bereavement, just an overwhelming sense of existential angst. Death was all around her. She worked with dead languages; was surrounded by portraits and busts of dead people. Maybe Denise was right. Death was following her around.

That evening, as she opened the fridge, even the lamb chops (dead animals) seemed to be accusing her. All right, all right, cauliflower cheese would have to do.

* * *

As the year turned, the days brightened and tight buds appeared on the trees, Emma's spirits lightened. She got out her bike, and gave it the once-over: oiling it and checking the tyres. At the weekend, she went for a spin round the local lanes. It was such a pleasure to coast down the hill with a warmer wind on her face. It would soon be time to get into the rigours of her spring and summer commuting routine. It was always an effort, but she knew that not only was regular cycling "good" for her, but that, as long as she could see where she was going, she enjoyed it. It wasn't the cold that had put her off cycling in London in winter – it was the dark. Far too scary.

And she needed to know where she was going. Off her own territory, Emma felt ridiculously insecure, and annoyed at being so. She wasn't a child, for God's sake. But it wasn't just cycling. It applied to every aspect of her life. She just wasn't good at uncertainty. For any trip, any conference, she made meticulous plans: tickets, location, weather, clothes – all had to be settled well in advance. Address, contact name and phone number. And her phone charged the night before. Any change to the arrangements flung her into disarray.

In London, drivers expected everyone to know the way, and if she didn't, she felt at their mercy; on an unfamiliar route, she was fearful of being driven into the gutter. She loved the idea of the new Quietways planned by the government, but for now she'd found her own. Even with the continuous upheaval of roadworks, she knew her way. From Victoria station, she only had to cycle a little way down Buckingham Palace Road, before turning into the byways of Eccleston Square and St George's Drive. Passing the back of the Tate Gallery reminded her every day of her intention to actually stop and go in. They had the occasional late evening opening – there was no excuse.

Cycling on the familiar side roads gave her a sense of freedom and belonging. She could almost believe she was a real Londoner, a real cyclist. How she wished that she could still use her own bike in London. It wasn't the same on a hired bike. Hired bikes were for visitors, for amateurs.

But with thoughts of cycling in London came the inevitability of passing that door. Even if she found an alternative route, she'd know that she was avoiding it.

Chapter 20

"Oh, and bring your glad rags," said Denise on the phone. "We're having a party on Saturday."

A party? "Oh, Denise, you know that's not my kind of thing. And, besides, I won't know anyone." A party was hardly what she had in mind. A coolness had remained since their Christmas altercation. Emma saw this visit as an attempt to put things right, but she was wary of opening herself up to more hurt, feeling that she had already betrayed too much of her fear.

"You'll know us. And you'll meet some nice people."

"Is Posy coming?"

"Well, I asked her, but she said she was on nights. Probably an excuse."

"Oh, I'm sure not."

Emma could almost hear Denise shrug. "Well, anyway, she isn't coming."

"But things are better between you now?"

"Well. We're talking, if that's what you mean, though there's a lot we can't talk about. I still don't get it. But her choice, I suppose. And it's probably just as well she's not coming."

"What do you mean?"

"Well, some people are coming that she might not approve of. Not saying more, but you're in for a surprise."

Emma's heart sank. What was her sister up to now?

But she had already booked her ticket and her time off work; it would be too difficult and time-consuming to change it now. And, besides, she was looking forward to seeing her sister's garden in its early spring freshness. She might even be able to take some cuttings. A bit early for most things, but perhaps that lovely fuchsia that she'd had her eye on. Denise would pretend to make a fuss, but Emma knew that her sister was seriously pleased that Emma asked her advice about something that she herself held so dear. However little she liked to admit it.

So, with a sigh, Emma picked out a frock that she quite liked, and tried it on to check it still fitted. It was a bit floral for today's tastes, but it would do. No one would notice anyway.

After her last visit to Dorset, Emma had finally caught up with Posy in London. She'd left it up to her niece to choose a meeting place. One of the problems with living so far out was that she couldn't easily invite friends or family home. Not that it arose that often – whom would she ask? – but it would have been nice to give Posy lunch at home instead of somewhere impersonal. But now that they were both in London, it made sense to meet in town, and Emma hadn't realised how complicated it was to find anything without gluten.

As it was a fine spring day, they had a little stroll in St James's Park before finding a salad place where Emma had given her niece the cake and toiletries. Posy smiled her thanks. Emma hadn't said anything to Denise, but she'd also worried about the safety of her niece. Everything one read in the papers about the darker side of London. All those stabbings, drugs, drink-fuelled violence. How on earth did Posy know what to do? And it was such an obvious target for terrorism. When she voiced her concern, Posy smiled in reply, and said reassuringly, "Honestly, Aunt Em, London's pretty safe. A friend of mine's lived all over the place, and says it's much safer than Rome or Boston. And it's surprisingly okay being a woman."

"Not sexist?"

"Oh, there's a lot of sexism, but not towards us. It's a really good team."

Emma had to admit it was reassuring to see her looking so well.

"I'm really happy, Auntie."

Emma could tell. Posy was glowing, and it was only when she was in a good mood that she called her "Auntie". Emma wasn't sure how she felt about it. She knew Denise disapproved, but she found it rather sweet.

She didn't think Denise had much to worry about. From the sound of it, Posy's intentions were philanthropic rather than authoritarian. She wanted to be of service, to train as a detective and specialise in child abuse. Emma didn't see her wielding a big stick. Posy's choice wasn't all about rebellion. She was her mother's daughter, after all.

* * *

Emma came down early for the party. As the sister of the host and a guest in the house, it seemed appropriate. The two of them had passed a pleasantly companionable afternoon making crudités, dips and other party snacks, and keeping off any subject that might be contentious. Julian was out for most of the afternoon. At work, Emma assumed, though it was a Saturday. He often worked unconventional hours. When he came in, at about 5 p.m., he was not alone. Emma could hear the murmur of voices, then the tread of several pairs of feet going up the stairs. In answer to Emma's quizzical look, Denise said nonchalantly, "He's just fetched some of the guests from the coach." It seemed odd that they didn't join the sisters downstairs. In fact, Emma couldn't help noticing that since she'd arrived Julian hadn't been his usual cheerful self, barely responding when she spoke to him.

"Have I upset him?" she now asked Denise.

"No, no, nothing like that." She tipped some olives into a bowl. "He's just got a lot on his plate."

The answer didn't really satisfy, but there was nothing Emma could do about it, so she tried to let it go.

Later on, as the other guests arrived, Emma sat in a corner, nursing a glass of white wine and feeling self-conscious in her flowery frock. Most of the other women, admittedly younger than her, were dressed more casually in tight-fitting jeans and low-cut or sparkly tops. Not for the first time, she felt out of place and wished she hadn't come. Denise too was in a frock. But it was a green wafty strapless affair that hung from a tight strap above her chest, revealing the tattoo of a seahorse. She'd always liked being noticed, but the tattoo had been done in her wild days, and Emma wondered if she'd regretted it – the fact of it, or the particular motif. Did she even remember what it meant?

But her sister looked pretty good, Emma had to admit. How did she retain that smooth creaminess of skin? Preferring the natural look, Denise didn't wear makeup (so last century!), except occasionally as part of fancy dress or when she wanted to shock. Which she managed very effectively with a red gash on her mouth and black circles round her eyes. Not that Emma herself ever wore much on her face. It was mostly for the mirror that she carried her mother's tortoiseshell compact. She never put anything on her cheeks – she wouldn't have wanted to block her pores – but she would have felt undressed without a bit of eye shadow and a touch of colour on her lips.

Emma looked around her. It all looked very festive: they'd had a cleaner in, and kept the lighting low. Without all the mess, it could now be seen as a pretty, well-proportioned room. Denise introduced her to one or two people, then was caught up in greeting new arrivals. Julian, circulating with a bottle of wine in each hand, gave Emma a wink as he passed. She ate, she drank, she exchanged a few words here and there, and wondered how long she would have to stay. At about nine o'clock, Julian raised his hand: "Hey, everyone, can you listen a minute?" And the hubbub died down. Speeches? Oh, well.

"And now," said Julian, "we have a surprise. We have a floor show for you. Please make yourselves comfortable, and welcome, all the way from Slovakia, the amazing klezmer group 'The Shadows' and their wonderful guest dancer, Veronika." The party guests turned to each other and clapped with surprise and excitement, some hurrying out of the room to relieve themselves, others to top up their drinks before the show began.

Emma didn't know what to expect. Denise's surprises were not always to her taste. She settled herself on her chair and hoped for the best. One young and two middle-aged men came into the room, carrying instruments – a violin, a clarinet and, with an effort, a double bass. Julian drew the curtains as the men settled themselves under the windows and began to tune up, and the audience, with a buzz of excitement, pulled up chairs, or sat on the floor against the wall. There was a moment of stillness, of breathless hush, and then the music began.

First of all, it was the clarinet alone: a disturbing, alluring sound, like the yearning of a human voice. It was unlike anything Emma had ever heard, and if she'd heard it on the radio, she'd have turned it off immediately. Too threatening. But, as it was, exposed to its seductive power, she had no choice but to be drawn in. She was caught, too, by the player, a small bearded man whose lithe body seemed to be part of the music, the clarinet almost like another limb. Gradually, she became aware that the strings had joined in, and the tune imperceptibly transformed from the woodwind's plaintive call to the rhythm of a dance.

Then from behind the audience a young woman came into the room and made her way to the front. Tall, stately, with dark hair streaming down her back, she wore a full-skirted blue dress, held in place by a black corset and with billowing layers of yellow underskirt. The shape of her body was hidden by the fullness of her dress, but the arms that protruded were thin beyond belief. With black strapped shoes tapping, moving almost in isolation from the rest of her body, she swayed first slowly then increasingly fast, holding her underskirts and rippling them like waves first in forward circles, then back. Emma was transfixed, caught up, in a bodily memory unconsciously straightening her back, lengthening the back of her neck, her feet moving to the sound.

In the dance, stamping, swaying, the young woman came alive. Her gold bracelets jangling, Veronika whirled, she shimmied, she covered the stage with ever faster intricate steps. Then she started clapping in time to the music, encouraging the audience to join in. Which, caught up in the energy of the players and the passion of the moment, they did.

As the group came to the end of their session, the rhythmic clapping of the audience turned into more sustained applause. The players bowed, then clapped Veronika, who stepped forward in acknowledgement. Denise and Julian bounded up to congratulate the players, Julian flinging an arm round the burly bass player – two big men in a bear hug – Denise beaming at the dancer, waving her arms as she expressed her thanks. Veronika gave her a quick smile, then turned to talk urgently to the rest of the group. The moment she stopped dancing, the poise and presence seemed to drop from her. Resisting even the offer of Denise's hospitality, she became edgy, anxious, a frail young woman eager to be gone.

As other guests rose to refresh their drinks, Emma stayed rooted to her chair, overcome by the experience. Her carefully guarded emotions, first churned up by the yearning power of the music, then galvanised by the rhythm of the dance, were in turmoil. The rhythm of the dance was coursing through her limbs. She was exhausted. She got up and made her way to the kitchen to fetch a glass of water before going up to bed.

As she drew near, she could hear raised voices. Actually, it was just one that was raised. Julian was as quietly spoken as ever. And the other voice, the woman's voice, was horribly familiar.

"Julian, will you tell me what's going on? What the hell are they doing here?"

As Emma paused tremulously on the threshold, Julian caught sight of her. "Oh, hi, Emma," he said. "Sorry, I've got to get those guys off to the coach." And, squeezing past her, he loped out of the room.

The woman wheeled round, revealing a pale, faintly freckled face beneath the brilliance of a copper mane. It was the girl.

The two women looked at each other in shock.

"Hello," the girl said, "I'm Nicola."

Emma and Nicola

Chapter 21

I had thought nothing could get worse. Just as I was beginning to recover a little, find my feet, however uncertainly, in a post-Phil world, I went to that bloody party. Coming face to face with that wretched woman again was almost more than I could bear. I felt the same kind of outrage as when I first saw her, when I caught her fiddling around with the flowers. Who the hell was she, and why did she keep popping up in my life?

Ian and I were late arriving, so I didn't clock her till Julian made his speech. I was still trying to deal with the sight of her when the musicians came through the door, and everything went pear-shaped. I recognised Martin the moment he came in, though once he started playing it was hard to believe it was him: that possessed clarinet player was nothing like the frightened little man who'd come to the funeral in borrowed clothes. Despite his promise to ring, I'd heard nothing from him, and had had no way of getting in touch. I was almost relieved to see him. I'd been in an agony of frustration at not knowing what he meant. What he knew. I couldn't wait for the music to finish so that I could get hold of him. Afterwards, I tried to draw him aside, but he waved me away, his eyes wild with what looked like fear, hissing urgently, "Not now, not here. I have to go. I will ring."

I collared Julian in the kitchen, but he was uncharacteristically evasive, and anyway that was when Emma came in. Like a bad penny.

It was all too bloody much. As if I hadn't enough on my plate. I was already wondering how to get out of there, but Ian was with me and, anyway, I could hardly turn tail in someone else's house. At least Julian seemed to have got the point and was doing something about it. I took a deep breath and tried to deal with what was in front of me. Come on, Nicola, she isn't stalking you, she's here for a reason. So I braced myself, and said hello.

"How do you do," she said in a small cool voice, "I'm Emma."

And then she started apologising. When I come to think of it, she did that the first time too.

I couldn't be doing with this. It was all so embarrassing. "No, please. Forget it. I overreacted. I do where Phil's concerned." I swallowed, and tried to be polite. "So... you've lost someone too."

"Yes. My... he used to be my boyfriend. A long time ago but somehow, seeing those flowers, I don't know why..."

I tried to acknowledge what she'd said, though it still stuck in my craw. "Ah. I'm sorry." After an uncomfortable pause, we turned to safer ground.

She turned out to be Denise's sister. I would never have guessed it: they couldn't be more different. And I still didn't see why Denise's sister should have been poking about with Phil's flowers.

She asked me how I knew her sister.

"Well, it's more Julian, actually. He was a friend of Phil's, supported the same cause." I took a breath. "Phil was my brother. Hit and run."

"How awful. I'm so sorry."

"Yes."

There was again a silence but it was warmer, somehow, shared, as if what we'd lost no longer got in the way, but formed a kind of bridge.

"I just wanted to ask..."

"By the way..."

We both started at the same time.

"No, go on," I said, "you first."

"That door..."

"Yes?"

We stared at each other.

"Did you...?" I began.

"What?"

"Put the flowers there?"

She seemed shocked. "No, no, of course not. I thought you had."

"No."

"What is it, that house?"

"I've no idea. I wish I did."

"Yes." She paused. "I was just passing, you know."

"Really?" Thinking of that pokey little street, it seemed unlikely.

And the question lay between us of why on earth she had got involved.

Then, perhaps out of embarrassment, she suddenly blurted out: "Did he have the same hair as you?" I couldn't see what it had to do with anything, but it was something to say. "Well, it was red, but a lot darker." I even smiled. "He didn't have people shouting 'Ginger' at him in the street."

Although I suppose it sort of helped to put a name to the face, and to discover, bizarrely, that she was Denise's sister, seeing her was a terrible shock. I simply couldn't work out what she had to do with anything.

Chapter 22

"Come on, darling, shall we make a move?" I was still standing in the doorway staring at nothing and didn't notice Ian until he was right in front of me.

"Oh, you made me jump! Yes, thanks, Ian. I'll just get my things."

In the car, everything was going round and round in my head. I'd obviously drunk more than I'd realised. Ian glanced at me. "You're very quiet, Nic. Anything up? It looked as if you were having quite an intense conversation in there."

"Yes, it was a bit. Can we talk about it later?"

"Of course."

I tried to gather my wits. "Did you enjoy it?"

"Ye-es. It's always a bit uphill when you don't know anyone, but it was good to meet your friends. I had a good chat with Julian. Interesting chap. A bit left wing."

"Oh, they're both that." As am I, but it wouldn't be politic to say so.

"I must say the music was great. I wasn't expecting that."

"Nor me." To say the least.

"I wonder where Julian found them. Slovakia, he said, didn't he? I thought klezmer was Jewish."

"Mmm. Don't know." I was desperate to change the subject.

"That dancer was terrific. Never seen anything like that outside of Eastern Europe."

"Here, Ian, turn left here."

"Oh yes."

We swung into a little drive and drew up at the side of the hotel where there were a few places for guests' cars. As promised, it was very pretty. A little old inn with a thatch, and in different circumstances the perfect venue for a romantic weekend. But I was desperately tired and, with all that was going on in my head, romance was the furthest thing from my mind.

Ian's a colleague, a bit older and higher up the scale. He's also recovering from a messy divorce, which was partly why I didn't want to burden him. At least, that's what I told myself. Ian is bright, funny and loving but occasionally plunges into periods of gloom, when he needs to be alone. We hadn't told anyone at work. It was too soon to be labelled a couple, and we both value our privacy: our evenings alone make what we have together even more precious.

I didn't know what Ian thought about Phil. Of course, they'd never met and I had to be careful about what I shared. I didn't want to upset the balance of our relationship with too much neediness or – heaven forfend – to make Ian jealous of how much I had cared for my brother.

Phil had been prickly but, like me, had been embraced by our parents. Even if they had never really understood either of us, we knew they loved us. Much as I enjoy my independence, I longed to recapture the familial warmth we had when we were growing up. But Ian isn't like that: he wouldn't live with me; he'd only just moved into his Barbican flat; he wanted his own safe place, away from prying eyes. But we were good together, and he was wonderful in bed. Imaginative, creative, caring of my needs. It was hard to give up on such a man and, after all, no one's perfect. I kept off the subject of children. I was getting needy in that direction, but it wasn't something I could mention. Not yet.

I have any number of good friends with whom I can discuss men, work, even family but none of them had really known the adult Phil. I had mentioned him, of course, but out of what I suppose is a sort of superstition, I had never shared anything about Phil's other life. Whatever he'd been doing seemed to be secret, after all, and in my heart, I worried that he might have got into something illegal. I simply couldn't bear to bring him into any kind of disrepute, and both did and didn't want to know what he'd been up to.

And I certainly couldn't share anything about all the odd things surrounding his death. It was all too personal. Even with Ian who, despite being a new man in my life, had been absolutely wonderful when Phil was killed. Didn't shy away from my anger even when I screamed with the pain of it all. He couldn't have been more loving and understanding. But this, this was different. Spooky.

And now that I had an inkling of what was going on, I absolutely knew I had to keep it quiet. I was scared stiff that I – or, even more likely, Ian – might be professionally compromised. After the shake-up in the civil service, he'd been moved to work on the post-Brexit migration policy. Although it was, of course, challenging, cutting edge stuff, I didn't envy him. Not my kind of thing. Anyway, work was farthest from my mind. I just didn't know how to deal with everything in my life. I felt overwhelmed by conflicting loyalties and also by an urge to share my confusion. It was so hard to make sense of it all. And Denise's strange sister turning up in the middle of it all – that was just the last straw.

Ian's comment about the musicians made me uneasy. Just because he didn't pursue it at the time was nothing to go on. He could be terrier-like in digging up the facts if he put his mind to it. I just hoped curiosity wouldn't drive him to find out. He was busy enough, God knew. I had also thought klezmer was Jewish rather than Roma, but discovered that there's some dispute about its actual origins. Giving a voice to the oppressed would do equally well for either, I suppose.

I'd written a journal on and off for some years. Life nowadays was mostly too busy for me to write much but since Phil's death, with no one to confide in, I had turned to my little book with a new resolve. I knew there was still a bit of self-censorship going on, but at least there was somewhere to put down some of what I was feeling. That turned out to be an understatement. As my anxieties poured out on to the page, my pen could hardly keep up.

Until the night of the party it was in the journal that all the turmoil stayed. But in the hotel bed that night wine spoke and I found myself telling Ian if not everything, then at least about how that wretched Emma had catapulted into my life.

"That woman I was talking to. I'd met her before. I couldn't believe it. She was there, where the flowers are... where Philip... She was poking about, she'd brought some flowers, for God's sake. What had it *got to do with her? I was going to put some fresh flowers there myself, but in the end, I couldn't bear to. And then, at the memorial service for road victims – you know – there she was. I didn't speak to her. I just ran. And then again tonight. I found out – she's Denise's sister. I just don't understand why she's always there, what she's got to do with anything."*

Ian pulled me to him. "Come on, darling, it's all over now. Come and give me a cuddle."

How I needed the strength of his arms. As we made love, I found myself responding with a pent-up passion that took us both by surprise. And, before I was aware of any separation, I was asleep.

Chapter 23

When Martin finally rang, his voice high-pitched with anxiety, I did agree to meet. My common sense urged me otherwise but, compromised or not, I simply had to hear what he knew. I had no idea where we could meet but Martin suggested a little Greek café in Camden, where no one was likely to know either of us, so we duly tucked ourselves into a little room at the back with Greek coffees and loukoumi. The café was pretty empty at mid-afternoon even on a Saturday, with just a few stragglers finishing a long and, judging from the empties, a pretty boozy lunch. Again, Martin took me by surprise. He had shrunk back into the pale and nervous man I'd first met, and it was hard to believe that that impassioned musician had ever existed. I was almost as nervous as he was, worried about being seen with him, but anxious above all to know the truth. "Please," I said, "tell me."

Martin sat on the edge of his chair and leant towards me. "I have to ask," he said in earnest and accented tones, "that you keep what we say quiet. It is dangerous for me to come today, but Phil did so much for me, I had to."

He looked pleadingly at me as, with heart sinking, I slowly nodded. "I Slovak, you know?"

I nodded.

"And Roma. We not liked. Many people in Slovakia, groups, they attack us. And my sister, Veronika, she klezmer dancer – you know?"

I nodded again. I'd guessed.

"She in danger in our country – bad men, they attack her" – he cleared his throat. "Much hurt. Police, even parents, they do not believe. So when she get job offer in UK, like a miracle. And man who offers, he is a sort of Roma so we happy. Then we hear nothing."

"She disappeared?"

He nodded, gulped. "Phil, he help us."

"How? How did he know?"

Martin tried to begin again. "As you know, I play in a band –

clarinet. Klezmer."

"Yes."

"Well, this is our Roma music, music played for many centuries, but we are not welcome in my country. So making public music is dangerous. We were invited to give concert in UK. St Ethelburga's — you know?" His face lightened.

Yes, I'd heard of it. In the City somewhere, not a church any more, but some sort of centre for reconciliation.

"You know Phil work for them as volunteer?"

"No, no, I didn't." I didn't know anything.

"He pay for us to come over, so I can try to find my sister. Phil help us, such a good man. We find her but we have to hide. Danger here and not legal, so...."

"No." I put my hand on his arm. "Please don't tell me." If I knew the details, I'd have to do something about it.

Martin studied me gravely. "Okay. Yes. But she must not go back." He took a swig of his coffee, and sighed. "We stay in England. Phil, he find somewhere; bring us food. Then... then he die." An electric pause. "But now Julian, he help a little."

Yes, Phil, he die. I was overcome. So this was some of what he'd been doing. No wonder he couldn't tell me. Stories of asylum were all too familiar; they were stories that in my line of work I'd heard hundreds of times, usually with an overlay of disbelief. Hearing this tale of devastation now, face to face in this scruffy little place, I felt the full force of the reality of Martin's life and the love he had for his sister. And maybe just a glimmer of why Phil might have died.

I suddenly felt a kinship: Martin's sister, my brother. My brother, who had cared enough for a stranger to risk his life. Thinking of the reports of increased abuse against foreigners, I said uncertainly, "I know people here aren't always kind." I fluttered my hands in an apologetic sort of way. "I'm sorry."

"No, no." Martin leant forward again. "People here so good, so kinder than people in my own country." How appalling, if that were true. *"It was our own people who took her."*

Another pause to absorb the shock.

He swallowed his coffee and jumped to his feet. "I need to go."

"Oh yes." I pushed my chair away from the table. "Where are you staying?"

"Better you not know."

"Oh, I mean do you have somewhere?"

"Yes, a tent. A charity gave to some of us. So," he smiled anxiously, "I am all right." He bowed awkwardly and left.

Burdened by my new knowledge, I paid the bill and slowly followed him out.

* * *

Ian was away and, for once, I was glad. Glad to have my flat to myself and relieved to be alone. Although I always missed Ian when we were apart, our times together were intense and sometimes I didn't have the emotional energy. Ian meant well, but in this instance he wouldn't understand. I wasn't sure I did either, actually, and I needed to have time to think. It was a particularly busy time at work, so it was precious to have a few hours to myself. Not least to catch up with my emails and personal admin. Working long hours, it was really hard to fit in things like getting the kitchen tap fixed, even getting a battery for my watch. Basic food shopping was okay. Even late at night, I could usually pick something up on my way home. But for the rest, I really needed a free Saturday to get it done. But not this week. By the time I got home it was too late.

So, as soon as I was in the front door, I kicked off my heels and loosened my hair. I like my hair. When I was in my teens, I tried to hide it – the bright colour made me stand out, and I didn't always like attracting attention – especially from creepy men who went on about it. Now that I'd had all these years to get used to it, I felt proud of it, and wore it long. In some ways, I felt it was a thing of beauty, almost separate from me. Ian called me his "Pre-Raphaelite" love but, unlike some of the others, he didn't get off on it.

Wanting to make the most of the last hour or so of daylight, I took a glass of Chablis out on to the balcony. I was so lucky with this place. Most of the flats on this Pimlico estate were bigger, for families, so to get a one-bedder overlooking the river, and high enough to get a panoramic view of the river and over the bridges, as well as a big arc of sky with birds and planes flying high and low, was an unbelievable piece of luck. Small it might be, but it was great to be so central, and so convenient for work. I could walk everywhere. Although I could see the flats in the block opposite, they weren't close enough to be intrusive, and at times like this it was such a solace to stand and stare, to just be.

When it began to get dark and chilly, I reluctantly went inside. I scrolled down my iPod for some Ben Webster – one of Phil's favourites and suitably melancholy – and took some vegetables out of the fridge to chop up for a stir fry. Always therapeutic.

I thought about the band. I was surprised, though, God knows, it was of no consequence, how pale-skinned most of them were. Was my assumption about skin colour a subtle form of racism? Having been brought up in a far-from-PC family, I am always alert for any form of prejudice in myself. Phil had generally kept me up to the mark, kept me in touch with what mattered. I would now have to do it for myself. Of course I always watched the news, knew what was going on in a broad sense but unlike Phil, in the world of work, my daily reality, I hadn't met destitution face to face, hadn't known how the other half – or rather the other ninety per cent — lived. Now, I could no longer claim that innocence.

I'm embarrassed to admit it, but, like most of my friends, any compassion I feel for people begging on the streets is undermined by irritation. I feel a mixture of helplessness and, if I'm honest, suspicion that if I gave money, I'd be had for a sucker. But a little voice sometimes says, "So what? You can afford it." One of my colleagues, who used to volunteer for a day centre in Victoria said that what people on the streets wanted more than anything was to be acknowledged. Even a smile would do. Makes sense.

In my heart of hearts, I knew that I have had a particularly low opinion of the Roma – those that my parents persist on calling gypsies. When I saw those young women sitting on the ground begging, often with a baby in their arms, I felt an impatience at their obsequious pleading, their form of emotional blackmail, even though I knew that some of them might be controlled, forced into begging. Now, I don't know. It's made me look differently at these often young, striking-looking women, so like Veronika, but with the life sucked out of them.

What I did know was that I was pretty fed up with Julian. He is so bloody thoughtless. He's a great bloke and all that and, for Phil's sake, I'm fond of him of course, but he just doesn't think about the consequences for other people. All the same, if I was going to really understand what was happening, I was going to have to ring him. Martin said he was helping. I'd been too caught up in hearing about Phil to think about it at the time, but now I wondered what form that help might take.

I sighed, and heated some peanut oil in the wok. As I stirred in the noodles and veg, I continued to ponder. I'd have to check the details of the legislation. Ian would know, of course, but there was no way I could ask him without rousing his suspicions. With even the little that I did know, I was surprised that the band had dared to show their faces in public. But I could see how much the music meant to them. Like an expression of their identity.

A clear picture of Veronika came up in my mind. What a lovely girl she was – and such a dancer. But she hadn't spoken to anyone, had seemed anxious to leave. I couldn't imagine what she'd been through or how she would recover, especially if she was sent back. It was unbearable to think that my colleagues, that Ian, perhaps, might be part of the machinery that would make that happen.

Maybe Martin was telling the truth about his reception here, maybe he was just being polite. If he had received kindness, I was profoundly glad; whatever the case, the system itself, as I well know, is not kind. It creates obstacles for desperate people and opportunities for exploiting those who have no other choice. Although, unlike Ian,

I'm not directly employed in the migration sector, I know enough to sense that the policies being developed are highly unlikely to be kind. Far from it.

I felt heavy with sadness. Had I finally reached my sticking point? Was this the end of the road? But I love my job. I still want to believe that I can make a difference. Keeping things from Ian was profoundly uncomfortable. There's only so far you can go in a relationship with secrets. Ian was my present and, I hoped, my future. Phil was gone. But what he stood for, the Veronikas of this world, were still vividly alive, and in need of help. However much I'd managed to brush such people under the carpet in the past, now that I'd met some of them, it was impossible. What a nightmare.

I scraped the veg on to a plate and, without much enthusiasm, took it to the table to eat.

Chapter 24

The following morning, I woke with energy and decided to make one last visit to the house. I was on my mettle. I'm not accustomed to funking things, and wanted to get it out of my system. Although it was broad daylight, I braced myself and took a heavy torch because, judging from previous visits, the stairs were still going to be dark and, though I mocked myself for the thought, carrying an implement of some kind made me feel safer. I had to face it: I was scared.

The Sunday morning streets were empty, so it took no time to get there. When I arrived, I found the door shut, but not locked. Feeling a bit silly, I knocked and eventually, and with trepidation, pushed it open, calling, "Hello?" The mean little hall smelt of disuse, urine and damp; the stairs were indeed dark and, as I went up, torch in hand, the rotting carpet squelched beneath my feet. My senses were alert for anything that moved. Especially rats. As I said, I'm not a fearful sort of person but the idea of rats makes my flesh creep.

At the top were just two pokey rooms and what might loosely be called a bathroom. The lavatory's seat was up, its bowl stained and the floor covered in cracked and dirty lime green lino. The place was hard to stomach, and I had to force myself to touch anything. I wished I'd brought rubber gloves.

For all the emotional buildup, my visit was a non-event. It was immediately clear that there was nothing to be found. A double bed filled one room, with a grubby sheet up at the window and a tangle of rumpled and discoloured blankets on the bed. Drawers pulled open with assorted bits of rubbish in plastic, bits of paper trodden on the floor – an old electricity bill, a couple of bits of paper with indecipherable writing in smeared ink.

In the other room were two dilapidated armchairs with God knew what dark grubbiness down between the cushions. From the open door of a peeling kitchen unit, I could see a couple of battered pans, and a few odd plates and bowls.

How could I have imagined that there would be anything of importance? It was unlikely that anyone who had spent time here would have had anything much to take. If there had ever been anything significant, it was long since gone; anything personal taken by its inhabitants or by those who had come through the ever-open door, and in any case the police would have found and taken any clues there might have been.

But in a sense, it wasn't a wasted journey. I had at least dealt with my fear and found, not the demons of my imaginings, but a sorry witness to the misery of desperate lives. A squalid place, yes, but one heavy with a presence of overwhelming sadness. I thought about the securities of my life, and felt ashamed.

At the same time, I couldn't wait to get home and under the shower, to wash the smell, the dirt, and the ugliness of that place out of my hair and clothes.

* * *

There was another visit that I couldn't avoid. We'd already had to wait weeks before the police gave us permission to clear Phil's flat, and the landlord was putting pressure on us to return the keys or pay another month's rent. If he had a middle name, it was not compassion. Ian had offered to come and help. It was sweet of him but I felt strongly protective of my brother's life, and his secrets. At the same time, it wasn't something I felt I could do on my own. The one person who was at the same time close to Phil and someone I could trust was Julian. I'd never felt completely at ease with Denise. She was a bit wacky for my tastes, and discretion was hardly her strongest point. But I felt confident that together Julian and I could tackle whatever we needed to do. I couldn't wait to get it over with.

Another door, another flight of stairs, again that tremor of apprehension. But this time the push of a button flooded the hall with light; this time I was on familiar ground, and I was not alone. The flat was bleak, but so different from those other rooms. Strangely, it had the feel both of somewhere that the inhabitant had just left and one that hadn't been lived in for some time. The air was fusty and stale, but on the living room table were what I assumed were the contents of Phil's pockets, just tossed there on a recent arrival: his passport, some loose change in another currency, and his Oyster card. I tried not to let the intimacy touch me.

The police had been there before us, of course, so there was no knowing how it had actually been when they'd found it. Knowing they'd been there unsettled me; it somehow tainted the preciousness of Phil's private place.

I tried to think if anything had changed since my last visit. I hadn't been there much – Phil had so often been away on a trip somewhere or other. The furniture was adequate, bog standard Ikea, typical of rented accommodation. As usual, there were four of everything: cheap white plates and bowls, spoons, forks and knives. Nothing to write home about.

Some of Phil's own possessions were achingly familiar. Hanging from the hooks in the hall were his coats: the big off-white greatcoat with an oil stain on the back; his navy fleece, a disreputable old anorak, and that flamboyant hat he'd brought back from Peru. From the same place was one of his few personal ornaments: the appliqué wall hanging with a crowd of embroidered trees, fruit, llamas and other animals. Otherwise, there were the usual bits and pieces, including a 12" TV, which I assumed belonged to the landlord. Phil's phone, I imagined, must have been with him at the time of the accident, either flung far from him or smashed on impact. The police hadn't mentioned finding it and it hadn't featured in his "effects".

They still had his computer, which they'd taken to check if there was anything that might provide evidence for what might still be a suspicious death. I hated them having it; hated them messing with what remained of my brother's life and the tangible evidence of his relationships. I was also uneasy that they might find something that they could consider suspect in his life or that might endanger others. Not for nothing had he kept some things under wraps. But he'd obviously been careful. Soon after the news of his death, I'd searched again for his blog, and it was nowhere to be found. He'd evidently deleted it, just in case.

Pride of place was the espresso machine that Mum and Dad had given Phil last Christmas. On the draining board were a couple of dirty little cups that showed that it had at least been used. I thought I'd ask my parents if I might have it, and then give it to Ian. It was more his thing than mine, and I didn't want to have to rearrange my kitchen to make room.

In a cupboard were a couple of new table mats – very untypical of Phil, but maybe he'd bought them as presents. They still wore tags of their origin: "made in Slovakia"; he'd travelled all over Eastern Europe in his gap year, but these looked as if they were of a more recent vintage. It was Phil's year of travel that had persuaded him to change to developmental studies at uni. I can't say the year politicised him, because he'd always had a political bent, but his views developed a sharper focus. And it was the voluntary work that he took on during that year that led him to the poverty action charity he ended up working for.

And then there were Phil's books. Travel guides, phrase books, Slovak and Italian pocket dictionaries, books on politics and philosophy, some of them evidently text books from university. Very little fiction, just the odd Frederick Forsyth to read on the plane and, touchingly, a battered little hardback of Shakespeare sonnets.

All in all, it wasn't much for a lifetime, but Phil had always travelled light. It wasn't just lack of money: possessions, he'd said "got in the way". As long as things ticked over, it suited Phil. He didn't want to think about the practicalities of his surroundings; the spark of his life had been elsewhere.

As we sorted through, I tried, without much success, to distance myself. Julian took charge of the clothes, folding them all into a holdall so that they could be taken to a charity shop: jeans, sweater and Phil's one good suit that he'd worn at Mum and Dad's anniversary party a few years ago. My parents hadn't asked for anything – they probably didn't know what he had – but I was on the lookout for anything they might like to have.

"What about you, Julian? Anything you'd like?"

Julian zipped up the holdall, stood up and stretched his back. He picked up the Slovak dictionary. "I quite fancy this. Looks interesting."

"Really?" Takes all sorts.

For myself, I took the Shakespeare sonnets and the Swiss army knife that I found in a drawer in the bedside table. It was something I recognised from childhood: a memento at least of our time together as a family.

I sat down heavily on one of the kitchen chairs, clasping my two little bits of Phil's life, and then the tears came. It was so hard, so unfair, so unjust. Julian came up to stand behind me and put his arm round my shoulders.

"Come on. I think we're done. Let's get out of here."

* * *

After all the trauma of recent weeks, it was so good to return to some sense of normality. Ian was back, home for the weekend, and at last we could find some precious time together. I couldn't think of anything better than Sunday morning with breakfast and Ian in bed. The papers scattered on the bed and on the floor.

"Coffee?"

"Yes, please."

"Croissants?"

"Oh, yes, please."

I don't usually bother with breakfast. Or, rather, I don't have the time. Although I live so close to the office, within walking distance in fact, I never seem to get up in time to do anything except wash, dress, grab my bag and run out of the door. So, what luxury that morning to wake not with a jolt to that wretchedly insistent alarm, but gradually, sensuously, with a body warm and replete from its nighttime adventures. Ian and I had been to a concert the night before:

the LSO and Brahms. I'd initially found the Barbican a rather sterile environment, and so hard to find my way around, but it was beginning to grow on me, and it was such an advantage to live over the shop, so to speak: at 10 p.m., as others rushed off to catch their tubes or trains, all we'd had to do was to trundle upstairs and fall into bed.

I stretched with pleasure. Ian had pottered out to the kitchen, naked as nature intended. He never bothered with night attire, even when he stayed at mine. I enjoyed the sight of his stocky, muscly back, and the way he walked – confident, assured, his own man. And someone, it seemed, who could allow me to be my own woman too.

"I've been thinking," he said as he carried a tray back into the room.

"Uh-huh?" I shuffled the papers out of the way.

Ian put the tray on the bed, and snuggled in to sit beside me. "Well, we've both been working very hard, and you've had a tough time recently, so I wondered about a holiday. I could do with a break too." I knew he was referring to his ex-wife. Although he rarely mentioned her, I knew she gave him a hard time. "What do you think?"

I was delighted. "What a great idea. Oh yes, let's! Where were you thinking of?" How wonderful to spend some undiluted time with my lovely man.

"I was wondering about Madeira. I saw something in the paper."

What bliss! It had been so long since my skin had felt the sun. Time for a top-up. I was longing for some warmth, for that greater intensity of light. That's when I come alive. Maybe I'm living in the wrong country.

Ian put a croissant on his plate: "I'd like to have gone to Turkey, but it's all a bit dodgy these days. Probably safe enough, but better to be careful."

"Poor Turks."

"Yes, and poor Greeks too. The whole business has ruined what was left of their economy."

I'd have been inclined to go there anyway, to support them in their struggle, but could see that Ian wouldn't want what might turn out to be a busman's holiday and I didn't want to rock such a promising boat.

"We'll need to see when we can both get away. So, shall I check out Madeira?"

"Oh, yes, please."

As we sat there, getting marmalade on the sheets, I felt as if I could go on saying "yes" forever. There had been too much gloom in my life lately. It was time to lighten up. Feeling almost guilty for being happy, I forced the reality of Phil out of my mind. The sadness was very real, but so was the happiness. It seemed, for once, that the two could co-exist.

Chapter 25

After the storms of her stay with Julian and Denise, Emma hugged her home and cats to her, and immersed herself in the reassuring routines of work. It was such a relief to get back to her own life. Normality had never felt so important.

That evening of the party, Emma hardly knew how she'd got up the stairs. She was dazed, bewildered. The music, the dance, but most of all the encounter with Nicola, had drained her, churning up all sorts of emotions that she didn't want to analyse. She had buried her head in the pillow and, despite the rising tide of now recorded music, in her little attic room she had slept.

The following morning had been Emma's last before returning home. Force of habit had propelled her out of bed at her usual hour and down to a scene strewn with plates and glasses, remnants of food and drink in all corners of the living room; the smell of beer and smoke filling the whole of the downstairs area. This time it was too much: she couldn't resist, and it was a way of calming her turbulent mind, full of unremembered dreams. At midday, when two dishevelled and hungover figures stumbled down the stairs, the rooms had been aired, the dishes done, and Emma was sitting demurely on the settee, a cup of tea in her hand. By the time she'd got on the coach, any vestige of a breach between the sisters had gone.

As spring expanded and the days lightened, the garden was beginning to demand more of her time and, as she dug and planted, bathed and slept, Emma noticed that she was beginning to feel both fit and more cheerful. Strangely, as the weeks passed, she found that the encounter with Nicola was no longer disturbing but in shining an explanatory light on the door and the flowers it had somehow dissipated their mystery. As time went by, she realised that her obsession had drained from her; that the whole episode had lost its potency. What a relief!

About a month after the party, Emma decided to test herself and cycle past the door. There it was, number 37, holding nothing of its former menace. There was still no sign of occupation, but neither were there any flowers or any gaping hole, just an ordinary scruffy front door like any other, in need of decoration. She could almost think she'd imagined the whole business. So what had all that drama been about? Just part of her general irrational behaviour? In any case, none of it was anything to do with her. It was for Nicola, poor girl, to discover what had happened to her brother.

Emma shuddered to think what the other woman must have thought of her. She was horribly embarrassed, but also felt purged – of that fear, and of all that ridiculous fantasy about Johnny's death. Shocking in itself, and devastating to her as it had been, he was gone. He was dead and buried, even if she hadn't been there to see it.

* * *

Easter was late that year. The daffodils, primroses and forget-me-nots were in full bloom, the camellias almost done. Emma didn't go away – there was too much to do in the garden – so she faced the holiday with a combination of pleasure at the thought of a bit of time at home and the challenge of empty days.

This time of year always reminded her of her mother, for whom it had had special meaning. She said that the middle day – Holy Saturday, she called it – was a time of waiting, a still place between death and resurrection, of breakdown and transformation. Emma didn't believe in the Easter story, but she couldn't help recovering something of the emotion absorbed in her childhood years. And as she walked in the garden, she couldn't fail to recognise it as a time of rebirth, and respond. It was spring, it was fresh; the days were lighter, the air warmer. The earth seemed to experience it. And the birds were awake. Even on the dullest day she could hear them. Every year she marvelled: it was as if life was beginning all over again.

For her mother's sake, Emma treated the holiday as a kind of memorial. On Easter Sunday itself, she kept to her mother's ritual. Slightly self-consciously, she put on a dress, tights, smarter shoes, and her little diamanté earrings. She boiled herself an egg for breakfast, dusted off the funny little sheep egg cosy that Denise, in a fit of whimsy, had given her, and sat with the papers, thinking, as she always did, that she ought to have gone to church. After lunch, she cracked open the Easter egg that Bob had given her. All that packaging. Denise would not approve. Emma removed the silver paper and consciously savoured the chocolate. How kind of Bob. How alone she felt.

The day passed pleasantly enough; in the afternoon she went for a walk; in the evening she cuddled up with the cats and, with only a faint sense of dissatisfaction, watched a re-run of Morecombe and Wise. At 9.30, she looked at her watch and sighed. She tried to feel enthusiastic about a bath and early bed. To delay the moment, she picked up the phone.

"Hi Denise. Happy Easter."

"Yes, you too." She had been drinking. Emma could always tell.

"Hope you had a good day?"

"Oh well, nothing special. Pretty idle. Stayed in bed, went for a walk, Had a drink or three. Nothing on the telly, as per usual. And you?"

"Much the same."

"Bet you didn't stay in bed!"

Emma smiled. "No, not that. The cats would make a fuss. But I did do a bit of gardening, which was nice. The plants grow so fast at this time of year."

"Don't they just? You're making me feel guilty." The sound

of a yawn. "Still, tomorrow's another day. If the weather's okay, we might go for a paddle."

It was the standard kind of empty conversation, probably being repeated up and down the land. But it was comforting in its way, and enough to settle Emma for the night.

She took her mobile out of her handbag to turn it off, and found that she had never switched it on. It happened sometimes – it was an old, non-smart phone, she used it only for messages and texting. Turning it on, she was startled to find on her voicemail a message from Nicola.

Hi Emma, it's Nicola. It was good to meet you (at last!) at Denise and Julian's. I was wondering if we could meet up some time? Maybe a drink after work? I gather you work in Lambeth and I'm just across the river, so it should be quite easy to find somewhere. Just give me a ring on this number. Cheers.

Emma couldn't imagine why they should meet and had no wish to. Any meeting would just recall her own embarrassing behaviour. She didn't even want to return the call. Thankfully it was too late to ring that night, but an ingrained courtesy forced her to do so the following day. Hoping to leave a message of polite regret, when Nicola answered and she was confronted with a spoken request, Emma was unable to refuse.

Chapter 26

The following week, Emma had an appointment with an eye specialist. When she had gone to the opticians for her annual eye test a couple of months before, she had dreaded what she might hear. She didn't want to know how much worse it was. But Mr Holly didn't think much had changed.

"To be frank, I think I should refer you again."

"Maybe," Emma said tentatively, "to someone else?"

"Moorfields?"

"That sounds good." Though she didn't see what difference it would make. The die was cast.

Waiting hadn't helped. First of all, the weeks of waiting for a date then, on the day, for a so-called 9.15 a.m. appointment, she waited till nearly 11 a.m. to be seen. Apparently, everyone's appointment was for 9.15. By the time she was called, her expectations were bleak.

But this time the nurse was gentler, the consultant kinder and when he examined her eyes, he said, "You know, you haven't got macular degeneration."

Emma looked up at him with astonishment.

"What you have is a macular pucker. Probably age-related. It won't get worse and while your other eye compensates, with some adjustment to your glasses prescription you should be fine. We don't need to see you again."

Emma didn't remember finding her way home. Discharged! Reprieve! In almost delirious shock, *not blind! not blind!* rang round and round in her head. She could see, she could read, she could work. She rang Denise, who was delighted, of course. But that wasn't enough. What could she do with all this joy? She picked up Perky, clutched her to her chest and spun round and round. She whirled, she waltzed, she danced! Letting Perky go, she turned on the radio. No matter what the music was

– it was some kind of jazz – she didn't think of it as music, more a prompt, a stimulus, an accompaniment to movement; she danced for all she was worth. When the piece finished, she fell, breathless and laughing, into a chair. She turned off the radio and, marvelling at herself, sat for a while, bathed in the lightheaded glow of a different self.

At last, gathering her wits, Emma rose from her chair and went to find Perky, who had taken refuge under her bed.

Dance! Yes, she was stiff, inflexible, old bones, but she could still respond to the joy, the music, the need of her body. Rhythm. It was irresistible. Only inhibition – that most English of qualities – had kept it contained for all these years. Well, no longer. The genie was out of the bottle. She kept before her the image of Veronika and that extraordinary dance, with hair and clothes streaming out into space. How the young woman had seemed taken up in it; how she had shrunk when the glory of the dance fell away.

By the next morning the ecstasy had subsided somewhat, but not Emma's resolution. In the hours and days that followed, Emma felt as if her eyes were open for the first time. It was as if everything had increased definition: the leaves on the trees, the cats' fur, the faces of people in the street. How was it that she had never noticed the uncurling of ferns in the spring? And not only her sight but her hearing and sense of smell. It was as if all her senses had suddenly woken up. She was filled with gratitude and a determination not to take anything for granted. She realised how, in anticipation of what had seemed inevitable, she had been shrinking her life. She needed to adjust her mindset to greater possibilities, to the wider world that was on offer. And she did not need to give up her work until she wanted to.

Strangely, though, now that she knew that there was no threat to her work, she felt paradoxically less involved in it. Despite her deep resistance, in the months of thinking she would have to leave, the bonds of attachment seemed to have loosened a little. Unwittingly, she had begun to let go. After all, she'd been working at the club for a long time. And there were other things in life.

Now that she was cycling less, Emma needed somewhere to put all her restless energy. For a long time gardening had been enough, but now she felt it was pedestrian, somehow. It took energy, but not of the expressive kind. She wanted something more, wanted to make more of being in London, and all it had to offer. Maybe she'd meet people too. Denise was into yoga in a big way – she'd been going for years, and was persuasive about its benefits. But from what Emma could see, it was all so passive, so slow – all that lying around. No, she could see the benefits for Denise, who said it calmed her down, but it wasn't for her. She didn't swim or play tennis. They'd neither of them been sporty girls – it hadn't been encouraged – and it seemed a bit much to start something from scratch. The one thing that stuck in her mind was, of all things, dance. It seemed a bizarre notion: at her age, with her way of life, her established sedateness. But she couldn't forget the magic of the klezmer dancer or the headiness of her own dancing on that extraordinary evening.

It was true that when she'd switched on the radio a couple of times and tried again, it had been a disaster. That was the problem, she'd been *trying*: she was self-conscious; the attempt had been prompted not by her body but by her thinking brain. That brain that served her so well in her career and all the doings of her daily life, was also, she could hardly bear to admit, a limitation.

Frustrated by her attempts, Emma's mind turned to the dances with which she was more familiar: the stately dances of the Ancient Greeks; stilted, maybe, but more appropriate to her age and standing. But even if there were classes for that kind of dance – and somehow she doubted it – that would mean other people. There was the rub. She both yearned for more contact with others and shrivelled at the idea of revealing herself in that way. It would involve touch, that childhood taboo. She had overcome it once; could she do so again? In a non-sexual way this time, maybe it would be less threatening.

Now that the subject of dance had caught her imagination, it was everywhere she looked. From the glittering vulgarities of *Strictly* to the Billy Elliot effect (the big poster for it at the Victoria Palace was something she passed every day). Even boys, who in the past would have been dismissed as sissies, were dancing. Not surprising, really – according to the evidence of Greek vases, they always had. Courtly, stately dance then, of course – a far cry from today's coarser practices.

Even Marilyn. When she had dropped into the office with Charlie, she'd revealed that she was taking up dancing: "Got to get this weight off somehow!"

Emma was avid for information. "Really? Good for you. What kind?"

"Belly dancing."

"*Belly* dancing?"

"Mmm." With a mischievous grin, she patted Emma on the shoulder. "You should come along, Emma. Do you the world of good."

"Hardly my kind of thing, Marilyn, as well you know."

The idea was preposterous, of course, but in one form or another, it seemed that everyone was at it. There was even research suggesting that taking up ballroom dancing reduced the chance of dementia. Something about creating new pathways in the brain.

Whatever the truth of any of this, there was no question that moving to music had made Emma feel alive. Even with her first step, she'd felt something loosen in her brain and in her heart: an expansiveness entering in, freeing a space of possibility.

But what kind of dance? She had no idea of where to begin. She'd heard of ballet for older people, but was repulsed by the idea of anything like the tight constraint of her childhood classes. How well she remembered them:

Saturday morning. Nine little girls spaced equally in a square room, bare except for a piano. Each girl standing sideways on to the walls, with their left hands holding the barre that ran round the room. Over the rather tinny sound of the piano the teacher shouts out instructions: *One, two, up, down, point your toe. Second position, no, Georgina, second position. Turn out, plié, and up. Face the barre, right foot on the barre. Straight legs, and point your toes.* Nine little girls of assorted shapes in tights and little dresses, straining towards perfection. One scrawny little girl straining more than the others, to prove to her mother that she's good enough to be there. As her little body stretches into one position after another, she creates straighter lines than the bumpy efforts of her plumper companions. For once her scrawniness is an advantage, and she does quite well.

At twelve o'clock prompt, the mothers arrive.

"Come on, Georgina, Jeanette, Emma, time to go home."

The discipline of those classes reminded her too much of the rigours of her adult life. What she remembered of those repetitive exercises had been like never going beyond scales on the piano and had little to do with the liberation she'd felt a few weeks ago and longed to experience again. But as she became more conscious of her body, Emma realised that, even in a ghastly tutu, those few years of ballet had been a beginning, had instilled something in her body, and taught her at least to be conscious of, and able to move, one part while others remained still – what did they call it? Isolation, that was it. That feeling of control brought her, in however small a measure, a sense of hope amid the turbulence.

But maybe because all those years ago it had been her sole expression of self, because she had *cared* enough to risk her mother's displeasure, dance was what had emerged now as a possible channel for her restlessness, relief from her bodily discomfort.

As a warmer energy tentatively filled the air, Emma began to breathe again. All that preoccupation with death seemed a long way behind her. Maybe there could, after all, be some kind of new life, for humans as well as the rest of the created world. More than ever, she longed to kick up her heels. Literally. She didn't, of course; she didn't dare let go of the sedate identity that she showed to the world and that even in her oh-so-private life was the only one that she would admit to. She couldn't escape the view of other people, even when there was no one there to see. If she didn't conform to that public persona, how would she know who she was?

One evening, as she passed through St Pancras station on her way back from a conference in Nottingham, she came across one of the free pianos being played with surprising verve and skill by an elderly man. Young travellers were gathered round, jigging on the spot, moving irresistibly to the music. Dance was all around her.

On the train home she dared to dream. It would have to be in London. There was nothing local to her and, besides, she couldn't risk bumping into someone she knew. Gorleigh Common was the place for her predictable domestic self; the library an expression of her professional capability; London, with all its massive disinterest, was an opportunity – for what? For letting go? Only in the anonymity of the city might she dare to allow her body a tentative freedom of expression.

Chapter 27

On the day of her meeting with Nicola, Emma set off for the café in a confused state. It felt odd to attend a social occasion in her work clothes. Her two lives – work and home, the visible and the hidden – were quite separate. Indeed, her hidden life was so concealed that it was barely visible, even to her. So, it was discomfiting to find the two lives entangled. She was also daunted. From what Denise had said, Nicola was seriously clever. Emma was sure *she* hadn't failed to get a First. So, maybe, Emma considered, it was just as well that the most private part of her private life was armoured in her work identity.

Nicola too was in formal work attire: even taller in high heels; the pink lapels of her blouse neatly exposed by the discreet neckline of a navy city suit. The two women faced each other over a small square café table, surrounded by laptops and oblivious figures plugged into their machines.

To begin with, awkward with each other, the two women indulged in small talk and, surprisingly, found that they had a certain amount in common. Although of different generations – Nicola was some years younger than Denise – they were both professional women and lived strongly independent lives. And had both been bereaved.

Eventually, Emma brought herself to ask, "How are you? Have you – recovered a bit?"

Nicola raised her head, and smiled a little, "Thank you, well, yes, I'm managing to work at least. That's a help."

Emma nodded. That was familiar.

"But it's so hard to believe he's gone. Men in the street look like him. I keep doing double-takes, whirling round to find that the man I've just passed is nothing like him."

"Yes, that that man you were so sure was him is wearing completely the wrong clothes."

"Yes, exactly."

Emma remembered it well, but also knew that for her it was a long time ago.

A slim young waiter with earrings brought their drinks. Emma thanked him.

"No worries," he said, as he moved on to the next table.

"I never thought there were," muttered Emma, flushing as she caught Nicola's amused response.

I didn't know how to frame the questions I wanted to ask. Although telling Ian had helped, and had certainly cemented our relationship, the meeting with Emma at the party had stayed with me. There was a feeling that what was important had been left unsaid. I still didn't understand, and couldn't leave it alone. But I didn't know how to broach it.

Sipping my wine, I said instead, "By the way, Emma, I think I know who put the flowers in that doorway."

Emma paused with her glass to her lips. "Oh, really?"

"Yes, you know that dancer at Denise and Julian's party?"

"You don't mean to say it was her?"

"I think it might have been, yes."

"But why?"

Nicola sighed. "It's a long story. Let's just say that Phil really helped her. She's Slovak, as you might know. And Roma, who aren't exactly well treated there. She was brought to the UK under false pretences, and probably doesn't have a legal right to be here. She was really scared about being sent back, so she had to disappear. So you see why she didn't hang around the other night."

Emma nodded, trying to absorb the horror of such a life. That dancer with her elegance and yes, well, *spiritual* presence, had not brought of any of her experience into her dance nor had she seemed anything like the shifty grubbiness that the word Roma conjured up.

Nicola was still talking. It's actually a problem for me,

because of the work I do. People simply mustn't know that she and I have met. Of course I didn't know she was coming, or who she was, in fact, although I'd met her brother – he was the clarinet player, you know. I can't think what possessed Julian to invite them. He knew it would put me in a difficult position. He and my brother were close; I guess he felt he owed it to Phil to help them. But he didn't have to be so public about it, or involve me. I'm really pretty angry with him."

"I'm pretty angry too, actually."

Nicola raised her eyebrows. "Are you?"

"Yes, but more with Denise, really. All this drama. It's so typical of her – why did she have to drag me into it?"

"Yes." Nicola paused. "But, actually, what did she drag you into?"

"Well, all this…"

"But meeting me, the house, the flowers, and so on – that had nothing to do with Denise, did it?"

Emma stared blankly at the other woman, then flushed and looked at the floor. She was right, of course. God knew where it had come from: all part of the ridiculous Big M fantasy. But, however irrationally, she still felt angry. This wasn't her kind of thing. She didn't get involved in this sort of nonsense. She didn't get involved.

She shuffled her feet under the table. "Well, and what about the house?"

Nicola shook her head. "I don't know. Some sort of a safe house, I think." They both sat for a while with their thoughts.

Nicola put down her glass and appeared to make up her mind: "Changing the subject, Emma, can I ask you something? I know how strongly you feel about RoadPeace, so I wondered… I don't know if you know, but this is the UN 'decade of action'."

Emma wondered what was coming.

"You may not know, but I've also been in touch with Brake, which campaigns for road safety too – to be honest, I've joined everything that's going, in case anything can help." Nicola gulped. "Anyway, there's a lot of excitement about Oslo's plans to ban cars from their city centre, and some people I know are joining a London demo in support – and generally anti-car, really. They'll have their own banner, of course. I'm wondering whether to go. Would you be up for it?"

Emma was appalled. "Me? A demonstration? I've never done such a thing. You should ask my sister." Who did Nicola think she was? Emma had seen marches and demonstrations on the news: ramshackle crowds carrying placards, shouting indecipherable slogans. The idea that she could ever be part of any such activity was beyond imagining.

Nicola leant across the table, her disconcerting eyes ablaze. "Come on, Emma. I don't go on marches either, you know; it's not exactly encouraged in my line of work."

Emma shrank back. "Oh, really? I just assumed..."

"The only protest I've been on was the anti-austerity one a few years ago, but that was just civil servants. No, I leave, left, it up to Phil. And Denise and Julian, who are brilliant. It's incredibly awkward for me. I can't afford to be arrested." *Although, feeling as I do at the moment, I wouldn't mind if my career did bite the dust. At least I don't have any dependents. I could retire to the country and have babies. Yeah, right! Fantasyland. But maybe causing a stir wouldn't be such a bad thing.*

"What the hell," I exploded, "he was my brother, dammit."

And Johnny had been Emma's love. The two women sat in silence, each contemplating the significance of what they might do.

Emma knew that, unlike Nicola, there was no reason for her reluctance, except her own distaste and, face it, her fear. She thought about the number of times Denise had taken her to task – about climate change, about refugees, about fracking – and she had never known how to respond.

"There's a big wide world out there. Don't you *care*?"

Of course she did. She just didn't see how marching would solve anything. "Why do you criticise my way of life? I never criticise you."

"Oh, you don't say anything but it's pretty damn obvious that you disapprove. You purse your lips and go all stiff."

That night Emma dreamt of Johnny. His back was to her, seen through a window, but it was recognisably him, in his tweed jacket. Throughout the day, as she went through the motions at work, some sense of loss stayed with her. She'd never dreamt much or, rather, she hardly ever remembered if she did. The Big M seemed to be stirring up all sorts of things, even in her sleep.

The next time they spoke, Emma made the mistake of mentioning her thoughts to her sister. "Maybe in some sense the dead are alive."

"Clever clogs," said Denise. "And maybe," she said, quick as a flash, "maybe some of the alive are dead."

Emma flushed and didn't deign to reply. Trust her sister to belittle something she was beginning to think might be for her a significant truth.

Chapter 28

The following day passed in a daze – Emma was tired and felt as if she were on autopilot. The day's work was full of unsatisfying bits and pieces, and travel exceptionally tiresome. Because of a cancellation earlier in the day, her morning train was unusually crowded though, unlike some of the other regulars, Emma managed to get a seat. As usual, the delay brought out a flurry of mobile phones:

"Sorry, trains are up the spout again. I'll ring when I know what time we're getting in."

"Sorry, I'm afraid I'm going to be late. Do start the meeting without me."

Emma remembered, when mobile phones first came in, seeing a man sitting on a station platform talking to someone, though there was no one there. She had made the assumption that he was someone with mental health issues who heard voices, and then she saw his phone. How times had changed!

Commuting was manageable as long as nothing went wrong. A work to rule, an excessive amount of rain or the wrong sort of leaves on the line sent everything into a spin, especially, it seemed, on Southern. On the whole, morning journeys were fairly quiet: people were waking up and not prone to lengthy phone conversations, and on the way home Emma tried to shut her ears. It was a short enough journey, and she knew she'd soon be back to the peace of her own home.

She was so glad that it was Friday – and still light. How she loved the long evenings! Even though she knew she was wasting an opportunity to be in the garden, Emma's Fridays were sacrosanct. She had to have a break some time, and marking the beginning of the weekend by sharing the evening with Bob felt like her own special time.

As they sat in the old man's sitting room, leaning back in

their chairs, the birds could be heard through the open window. They too were celebrating the beginning of summer.

Bob seemed to be reading Emma's mind. "Ah, my dear, what a pleasure it is to share this time with you. How long have we been doing this?"

Emma considered. "Fifteen years or so? A very long time."

"Yes, it has been an important part of my life. I'm so sad that there won't be many more evenings like this."

Emma sat up. "Why? What do you mean?"

"I'm afraid I'm going to be moving."

Emma was aghast. "*What?* Where?" She swallowed. "Why?"

Bob laughed. "So many questions. As to why, that last turn I had really put the wind up me. It made me realise that I needed to take better care, and my daughter has been saying that for a while now, saying I need to be closer to her, so that she can keep an eye on me – and she's right. She's found a really nice place near where she lives, in sheltered housing. We're just waiting for a space. They thought it wouldn't be long. Alice has had a look at it, and she's going to take me to see it soon."

"So it's in London? Oh, Bob." Emma was disconsolate. "How I shall miss you."

"And I you, and this little place. This life." Bob looked round the room, and sighed. "But *anno domini*, you know. Catches up."

It was true. She'd been lucky to have him so long.

Bob smiled at her. "And you're in London anyway. You could always come and visit me."

"But it won't be the same."

"No, it won't."

At the end of the evening Emma let herself into her house with sadness in her heart. Dear Bob, what a good companion he had been. Her mind ran on. Goodness knew who she'd get next door now. How hard it was to face change. She stopped herself. Come on, Emma, it's much harder for Bob. Think of it: having to give up so much – everything he's known and most of what he has – but, true to form, he wasn't complaining. Like the best of the Greeks, in misfortune he was not one to rail against the gods.

She wondered whether, sub-consciously at least, the impending change had been at the root of his choosing Marcus Aurelius for their next book. How appropriate were the stoicism and far-sightedness of what they had read that evening:

It is not right to vex ourselves at things

For they care nought about it...

If gods care not for me and my children

There is a reason for it.

For the good is with me and the just.

No joining others in their wailing, no violent emotion.

Emma sighed, and began to go through the motions of closing the house down for the night. Pulling down the kitchen blind, drawing the curtains, switching off the lights. Before turning off her phone, she checked it for messages as usual, and found that there was another voicemail from Nicola.

"Apparently, there's going to be a flashmob dance. Wow! What do you think of that? Don't worry, Emma, apparently you just go with the flow."

There was a pause.

"Emma... I will if you will."

So Nicola was serious, then. Oh dear. But what on earth was a "flashmob" – was that the word? Emma felt as if she were penetrating even further into alien territory. She looked at her watch – they'd still be up. There was only one person she dared ask and even asking her was a risk, so she was glad to get Julian on the phone. She could be sure he wouldn't sneer.

His voice was amused. "Flashmob? Goodness, Emma, what are you up to?"

"Oh, nothing, Julian. I just came across it and wondered."

"Well, a flashmob is a group of people who do something unexpected at a mass event, like a demo or a celebration. I've only been involved in one about nuclear weapons, where we all suddenly put on death masks."

Death masks. Again. Emma stopped listening.

"It was really powerful. But there can be dance, singing – there was a great one in a Waitrose once, just for entertainment – and a friend went to a meditation one in Trafalgar Square. There are usually one or two people primed to start it all off, and everyone else pretends just to be acting normally until the signal is given. It's great fun. Emma?"

"Oh, yes, sorry. Thanks, Julian, that's really helpful."

Emma put down the phone and stood still. What had electrified her was the word "dance". Just now and in Nicola's message. And everywhere else, it seemed.

Emma was unsettled. She paced up and down the darkened rooms, raised the kitchen blind and stared out at the night sky, at tall trees outlined against dying streaks of red. Nicola could not have known about her deep-seated longing, or that for her dance was already, had always been, the language of protest. Was it possible that she would now put that into action? That years of impotent grief could be expressed at last in a common cause? A cause worth marching for. In Johnny's memory.

Finally, with an air of decision, Emma took her torch from the kitchen drawer, put on her boots, picked up the compost bin from the kitchen, and made her way carefully down the garden path. Remembering the time when she brought sunflowers to a vacant house, that time when it all began, she carefully scooped out a few seeds from some now dead sunflowers, and laid them on the kitchen windowsill to dry.

On Saturday she would put them in a little plastic bag, and put that bag in her handbag. When she was on the march – on the march! – only she would know they were there.

Chapter 29

Julian was always hard to pin down. Probably not intentionally, but he worked odd hours and didn't always answer the phone. I didn't want to say too much to Denise, in case she didn't know. I wasn't keen on this cloak and dagger stuff, but in this case, I had a sense that there were secrets that needed to be kept.

So I was pleased when Julian texted me.

Hi Nicola, Hope all's well. 'Fraid I won't be coming to the demo on Saturday. Fact is I stupidly tore something in my knee when I was running last week. The meniscus, apparently. So I've got to rest it. Really sorry to miss it, but it's also a bit of a relief not to have to come up to London. You know how I hate it. Anyway, Denise is still going on the march – you wouldn't keep her away – and I just wondered if you could keep an eye on her. You know what she's like. Sorry to be a bore. Come down and see us soon. J.

Hi Julian. Poor you. Hope it's not too painful. How long will it take to heal? What d'you mean: "you know what she's like"? Sounds sinister! Look after yourself. Nx.

Oh, forgot you haven't been on demos with us before. She can get, well, carried away. Last year I had to sweet-talk a copper to stop her being arrested when she kicked him on the shin. She was furious – wanted to be arrested. Better credentials, you know, brownie points. So, keep an eye on her, would you? J.

Oh, Julian, do me a favour! There's a good reason I don't go on demos. I have to keep my head down. I'll do what I can, but I'll have my work cut out watching out for Emma – you know she's coming too? Scared stiff, poor lamb. I rather pushed her into it, because RoadPeace is her thing. Nx.

Emma? You're kidding! Bloody hell! Wait till I tell Denise. Got to get on now. Promised to help plan our solstice do. We can't go to Stonehenge this year because of my leg, so we're inviting some people over here. We'll probably go down to the beach – should get a good view if the weather's decent, Have a bonfire, do some yoga, all that. Why don't you come? Should be a good crowd.

Yes, it would be lovely to be by the sea, but I couldn't think of anything I'd like less than one of Denise's wacky dos.

How kind, but no can do. Work day and all that. Sorry. Hope it goes well.

Actually, I was going to ring you. Something I need to talk about. When would be a good time? Nx.

Needless to say, Julian didn't reply. I grimaced as I left the computer. I was beginning to regret the whole thing. Not only had I not got any answers but I'd got lumbered into the bargain.

Chapter 30

The phone went when Emma was in the middle of supper. It was Denise. Perfect timing, as usual.

"Hi Emma, you okay?"

"Yes, thanks, just eating."

"Oh, sorry, won't keep you long. Nicola told us you're going on the march on the seventeenth. Are you really?"

Emma bridled. "Yes, I am, actually."

"I'm amazed. That doesn't sound like you. But I'm delighted, of course." Denise laughed. "We'll make an activist of you yet!"

"Hardly." All she wanted to do was get on with her meal.

"But I'm curious. How do you know Nicola?"

Emma hesitated. "We met at your party."

"I know, but..."

"Hang on, I think Pinky's being sick."

"Oh, you and your cats!" – but Emma had put the phone down to get Pinky out of the back door before the retching led to a concrete result.

"Sorry, where were we?"

"Nicola..."

"Oh, yes," said Emma, thinking quickly, "and before that, we'd seen each other at the RoadPeace service." No less than the truth.

"Ah, so that's it."

"She told me about her brother."

Denise sighed. "Yes. Poor Phil. That was a terrible thing. Shocking. It'll take her a while to get over it. They were very close. Julian too, actually. They were very good friends. He was gutted not to get to the funeral."

"I'm sorry." Maybe that was what had been on his mind.

"And it's harder when there's a question mark over it all."

"Question mark? What do you mean?"

"Oh, I don't know, just something Julian said."

"What? Come on, Denise, stop being mysterious."

"Well, Julian thought that something Phil was involved in might have been a bit risky. Someone might have wanted it stopped."

Not another conspiracy theory. "Oh, come on, Denise, that's a bit far-fetched."

"I'm only telling you what Julian said."

Emma doubted it. He was the sensible one in that relationship.

"You're such an innocent, Emma. Bad things do happen."

Emma bristled. "Don't patronise me. You're always so melodramatic; it's hard to take you seriously."

"Thanks a bunch."

"Anyway, I must go. My food's getting cold."

"Oh yes. Sorry." She didn't sound it. "See you on the seventeenth then?"

"You'll be there?"

"Of course. We've got a big Green group going. But you've heard about Julian?"

"What about him?"

"He's done in his knee, so can't come."

"Oh, I'm sorry. I hope it gets better soon."

"Yes, it's a real bore," said Denise somewhat unsympathetically. "But I'll be there."

"Good. Though I can't say I'm looking forward to it. I don't like the thought of all those people. You know me. I'm not good with crowds."

"Don't worry, we'll tag along at the back where there'll be less people."

"Fewer," said Emma automatically.

"Oh, Emma, don't be so snobbish."

"It's not snobbish to want language to be used accurately."

"Oh, pedantic, then."

"Well, maybe. But you wouldn't like someone to play

something out of tune, would you? You'd complain."

"I suppose. But language is a living thing. Not stuck in some long-dead culture."

Emma put down the phone. Then, as she marched over to the cooker to heat up her food, feeling the familiar uprising flush, she reached over to open the window, put her hands flat on the worktop and forced herself to stop. Why couldn't they have a conversation without bickering these days? In the past she'd learned not to comment when her sister made snide remarks, especially about her work. She knew there was no point. Denise had never understood and, yes, if pedantry meant a concern with correctness, with order, then she was pedantic, and proud of it. She cared about grammar, accuracy and the placing of apostrophes. *Standards*, she could hear her grandfather say, *you've got to have standards*. Not something Denise would understand. Fortunately, she herself worked in an environment where these things did matter. It meant a great deal to her in her work and in her life, to be orderly.

* * *

For most of the week before the demo, I worked late. There was nothing new in that. With so many caught up in the ongoing task of what our former chief, Gus O'Donnell, had called "the massive task of making Brexit work" the rest of us were chasing our tails just to keep everything else ticking over. Ian was up north, I had nothing to rush home for and, having eaten lunch at my desk, I decided to give myself a break and walk down to St James's Park. It was still light: nearly Midsummer's Day, I realised. It's always hard to accept that from June onwards the days start getting shorter. Whatever it's called, real summer had barely begun.

It's on long summer nights that I really miss the countryside, the beauty of the spacious land that I grew up in, and the fresh green of new growth. The lambs, the freedom. Memories of that swing we had on the farm, when I'd felt as if I was sailing over the fields and into the sky. Perhaps once the demo was over, I could persuade Ian to come with me to a country pub. Away from the nitty gritty, giving ourselves the chance to stretch out into the open spaces.

Of course when I think of a place that I miss, I always remember it in the most perfect weather! A sunny July day with a blue sky, green grass, and golden crops ready for harvest. Not a sodden muddy bog fit only for the heaviest of Wellington boots. Stuck in the city, I sometimes long for an idyllic trip to the seaside or out to the country, forgetting the hours in a friend's car spent bumper to bumper on the motorway. We obviously need to imagine only what we yearn for.

Anyway, even when I hanker after the countryside, I can still appreciate the city. Most people I know have a similar ambivalence: they're not content with either; they want a bit of both. At nine o'clock there were plenty of people about, taking advantage of a night warm enough to sit out with a layer or two. I walked on to the Blue Bridge and watched a duck proudly leading half a dozen of her brood as they paddled by. I gazed across the water. Behind Horse Guards Parade and my colleagues' offices in Whitehall, I could see, on the other side of the river, the London Eye, no doubt full of people on a clear evening like this. I'd been snooty about it when it went up, but I really enjoyed the time I went on it for a friend's birthday do. Such a view of London: made me proud to feel part of it. I might crave the wide horizons, but this is my adopted city. On good days I do love it.

Especially the parks: they're such a great part of London. Even on a hot evening you can find a quiet corner under a tree and away from the snap-happy tourists. (As a resident myself, albeit of not very long standing, I can afford to join Londoners in feeling a bit superior.) You can actually cross the city by walking through one green space into another. And, although central London isn't as compact as Paris, it's surprisingly walkable. When I was a child, all our travel in London was by tube, popping up in one place or another without any notion of the connection between them. When I lived here as a student, I couldn't afford to nip on and off the tube, and so I discovered the delights of walking and the intimate realities of this vast city.

My saying that it had probably been Veronika who put the flowers on the door was guesswork really. But who else could it have been? I did wonder how on earth she – as a hidden person – could have got the flowers. Stolen them? That would make sense of the fact that the flowers were obviously from someone's garden rather than shop bought. But what if she'd got caught? It was a hell of a risk. It didn't bear thinking about.

I thought again about the demo. Why am I doing this? My career is precious to me, and hard fought for. Mum had never understood why as a woman I would want to work. And it's not just my career that I'm risking, but my relationship. I feel bad that I can't share news of the demo with Ian. He probably wouldn't approve, and I simply can't risk it. In his new position he has to be even more careful. He's also more conservative than me – he doesn't belong to a union for fear of divided loyalties. I've got less faith in the powers that be – even less after recent events. If I get into hot water, I'll need the protection of the FDA. I'm beginning to realise that my misgivings about work are mirrored, however little I like to acknowledge it, in those I have about Ian. Not surprising, really since he identifies so strongly with what he does. I'm trying to get to know the Ian beneath his work identity which was, let's face it, what brought us together. With a broken marriage only just behind him, it isn't surprising that he's focusing on the bit of himself that he knows works. He is very good at his job. Maybe the holiday will help bring us closer.

I'm doing all this for Phil, of course. And, in a funny sort of way, I don't want to let Emma down. Although I barely know her, we have a sort of connection, and I am touched by her timidity. Emma's not much older than me, and hardly the motherly type, but I feel strangely drawn to confide in her. My own mum is too immersed in her own grief to hear anything of mine, and our memories of Phil are too different. I've never felt so distant, and can hardly bear to visit. Feeling guilty, I keep up my weekly phone calls and listen to her talk of other things and trying to be brave, and I always feel depressed when I put down *the phone. We just have nothing to say to each other. Dad might be better, but he hates talking on the phone. So it is with a strange sense of relief that I talk to Emma.*

I've often wondered what it would be like to have had a sister – as a family, we're remarkably short of female relations – but while Phil was alive I hadn't really felt the lack. My women friends were enough and now, goodness knows, they're a godsend. I know Denise much better than Emma, of course, but she doesn't know at firsthand what I'm going through and we've never really been close. Besides, she and Julian are so absorbed in each other that it's hard to get an in.

To my surprise, given how troublesome she was to begin with, the bizarre way Emma expressed her grief feels like something I can relate to. It's the extreme unreasonableness of her behaviour that chimes with my own fury and grief. Somewhere in that prim tight little body is a passion that matches my own. I realise that it was not the smell of death that made me run from her, but the fear of a contagious unreason. So, not a mother, not a sister, maybe, but a mad little maiden aunt.

But for the next step I know I'll be on my own. For me, this protest is just the beginning. Phil had been a road victim, yes, but a victim of more than that, and a representative of all those other victims for whom he had fought and, in the end, lost his life. If I am to be true to his memory, I will have to go deeper, and goodness knows where that will take me. Stop the traffic, yes, and stop the traffick too.

Chapter 31

In the meantime, I did need to get hold of Julian. I waited till after the solstice before trying to ring but when I finally did get through, he was cagey.

"I'd rather not do this on the phone."

"What do you mean?"

"It's just, well, complicated and a bit sensitive."

I wondered whether it was something he was keeping from Denise. "Oh dear. Yes, I suppose. Well, what do you suggest?"

"Is there somewhere we can meet?"

"It would have to be at the weekend."

"Yes, it's such a bind I can't make the demo – that would have been the obvious time. Though it might have been hard to get some time on our own."

"Yes." Hmm.

"I'm afraid I'm just not very mobile."

I was beginning to get irritated. "Well, Julian, much as I'd like a day by the sea, I simply don't have the time."

Julian paused. "Tell you what, I'll ring you back a bit later. Maybe hobble out somewhere."

So it was Denise. "Okay, that's fine."

When Julian rang back an hour later, I could hear the sound of the sea.

"Yeah, on the beach. Denise had some students coming. I just didn't want us interrupted."

All this secrecy was so unlike Julian. He's a straightforward sort of man. Rather endearing that he was so bad at lying. I wondered whether to tackle him. But what would be the point? If he was keeping something from Denise, it was hardly my business. And Veronika was a very pretty girl.

"Anyway," he said, "it's Veronika. She's in a terrible pickle."

"I gathered that. How does she come into the picture?"

"Well, you know Phil met Martin in Slovakia?"

"No, I didn't even know he'd gone. He kept his cards quite close to his chest."

"Yes, he went on a fact-finding mission to Eastern Slovakia for the EU, oh, some years ago now. Anyway, when he visited a Romany encampment, near Rudnani, I think he said, Martin collared him and told him his sister had disappeared. She'd been attacked, abused, by a group of youths near their home, so her arranged marriage fell through – the boy wouldn't take her on. So when she was offered some kind of job in the UK – it came from a different Roma group – osada, I think he said – whom her family didn't usually talk to – it felt like a God-sent opportunity.

"But once Veronika got on the plane, there was silence. Martin was out of his mind with worry, Phil said. As you know, for Roma, family is everything."

"Yes." That much I did know.

"Anyway, Phil, like some knight in shining armour, tried to track her down in the UK, but of course it was hopeless. They had no idea where she could be."

"How terrible."

"And then, out of the blue, months later, Martin heard from her. Apparently, she spotted her employer's mobile lying on a desk, and took the risk of phoning him. It was only a few words, as you can imagine. She was nearly hysterical, Martin said. Apparently, there were some Roma at the airport to meet her, so when they asked for her passport, 'for the formalities', she wasn't suspicious. But she never got it back, or her phone. She was driven to somewhere on the outskirts of London and became what I think is called a domestic slave. With no money or papers, and next to no English, she was trapped."

"My God."

"Martin called Phil, who somehow wangled an invitation for Martin and the group to come over to the UK to give a concert. God knows how."

"Apparently, Phil was volunteering for the place they played at."

"Oh, was that it? What a bloke. Anyway, amazingly, he and Martin managed to rescue her. Martin was too incoherent to explain exactly how, but something about a shopping trip – the people in the house had no suspicion that she could be found – and then she and Martin had to go into hiding." Julian paused.

"I can't believe it. In this country!"

"It happens, Nicola. You know it does."

"It's so appalling." There were no words.

"Yes, well, then Phil, who I think was in love with her by this time, tried to find somewhere where she wouldn't be found. A safe house, I suppose."

I had a strong suspicion of where that was.

"But eventually, I guess, they caught up with him."

My worst imaginings. I was flabbergasted. "Julian, do you really think so?"

"What else?"

"But we must go to the police."

"Veronika won't – she is so scared the gang will catch up with her or that she'll be sent back. Her experience of the police doesn't make her trust them, even here. And not even the big agencies like the Refugee Council, the Sally Army – Martin says they're hand-in-glove, rely on government for funding, have to toe the line."

"But why should she be sent back? Surely trafficked victims are protected?" But I knew as I spoke that women like her, even if they have the courage to come forward, are rarely believed.

"God knows under the present system. You'd know more about that than me. We still lock them up."

I couldn't deny it.

"And, anyway, she hasn't got any papers, no proof of who she is or where she's from."

"What a nightmare. The poor woman." I tried to think about the details of that recent statelessness legislation. Maybe that's what Phil had cottoned on to. Maybe that was what might have offered a glimpse of hope. But now, of course, everything was up in the air.

"I think Phil was beginning to make her feel safe. I think he was finding a way – and now…" His voice petered out.

Yes, and now, Phil, he die. No wonder Veronika had left the flowers. She had even more reason than me.

"Julian, do you know where she's staying?"

"Well." He hesitated. *"Well, yes, I do, but no one else, not even Denise. I had to promise. It used to be Phil, now it's me. You saw how Veronika was. All I can say is that she's moved out of London, north. It felt safer. Some of the group know, I guess, but they won't trust anyone else. It must have taken quite something for her to trust Phil. He told me very little. I think he didn't want to put me in danger. I just knew he would want me to look after her. I got a message to her through Martin who is himself scared, as you could see, and he feels so bad that he hasn't protected her. But at least I had his email address."*

"But what are we going to do? If not the police, then what?"

"God knows. She'll need new papers, of course."

"What do you mean?" My professional hackles rose.

"Well, she doesn't have any."

"But you don't get them just like that. There's a hell of a procedure."

"Yeah, that's what I mean."

As I put the phone down, I had a strong suspicion that Julian was planning something he knew I wouldn't like. I noticed that I had used the word "we". He seemed to be assuming that I was going to help. How could I not? Maybe it was partly guilt at my previous attitude to Roma. But I had no idea what we could do. Nothing nefarious, that was for sure. It would be more than my job was worth. I couldn't check with Ian – it was too dangerous – and I couldn't think of anyone else I could safely ask. I could support Slavery International, Stop the Traffik, any number of organisations, but what really needed to happen was a change in policy and maybe, I thought with a sinking heart, that was where I came in.

My poor darling Phil. No wonder he'd felt unsafe that time we'd met in the pub.

Then I remembered something with a jolt. That phrase that Julian had dropped into his account. In the horror I had almost missed it. "Phil, who I think was in love with her by then". In love? Her lover? How did Julian know? When was it going on? Was Veronika my lovely brother's love?

In turmoil I wandered out on to my balcony. Some small boys were playing with a football between the flats. On the road along the river, a bus went by, and on the river itself a tug was making its way towards the bridge. Normal life.

Trying to distract myself, I got out the ironing board, then remembered that I hadn't arranged a time to meet Emma for the demo. I'd had enough of phones for the evening but knew she was unlikely to pick up a text. Why couldn't she be on email like the rest of us? With a sigh, I picked up the phone.

Poor thing, I could tell she was nervous. Perhaps I shouldn't have pushed her into it. Before we rang off, Emma asked if there was any news of the dancer. "Veronika, wasn't it? What's she going to do?"

"I wish I knew."

"I asked Denise, but she didn't seem to have any idea."

"No, it's more Julian."

"But why? Why has he got involved?"

"Feels he owes it to Phil, I suppose. He's the sort of person who just does get involved."

"Yes, he is. Never understood it, really."

There was a pause, then Emma said abruptly, "Nicola, do you know Posy?"

I was a bit irritated at the sudden change of subject. "Posy? Who's she, when she's at home?"

"She's my niece, Denise's daughter."

"I didn't know Denise had a daughter."

"Yes, she's a really nice girl. She's just become a policewoman."

I was gobsmacked. "A policewoman? Denise's daughter?"

Emma gave a short laugh. "Yes, a bit of a shock, as you can imagine. But I thought of her because she's talking of specialising in trafficked women."

"Is she now? How interesting."

Emma obviously felt that she'd said too much. She stammered, "I only meant... I mean she won't know anything yet. She's only just begun."

Nonetheless.

I shrugged and echoed Julian's remark: "God knows."

* * *

On the morning of the march, I woke with a head full of cold. How good it would be to surrender, to stay in bed and bury my head and my conscience under the bedclothes.

Metropolitan Police

1. On today's date, Detective Inspector Gunnell brought me a laptop computer running Windows® 10 that had been removed from the home of a victim of a hit and run incident. A full forensic examination was requested to see if there were any documents that could help the inquiry into a possible suspicious death.

2. On today's date I began the forensic acquisition/ imaging process of the laptop. Prior to imaging the laptop, I photographed the laptop, documenting any identifiers (e.g., make, model, serial #), unique markings, visible damage, etc., while maintaining chain of custody.

3. Using a sterile storage media (examination medium) that had been previously forensically wiped and verified by this examiner.

4. At this point, I removed the hard drive from the laptop and connected it to my hardware write blocker,

---

which is running the most recent firmware and has been verified by this examiner. After connecting the hardware write blocker to the suspect hard drive, I connected the hardware write blocker via USB 2.0 to my forensic examination machine to begin the forensic imaging process.

5. After completing the forensic acquisition of the laptop I began analysing the forensic image of the laptop with Forensic Tool.

(There then followed a list of forensic tools employed.)

6. Among the documents recovered was the following draft, written over a period in July 2016.

Ghost-rescue UK (GRUK)

The UK, Europe and the rest of the affluent West are full of ghosts. People who are accepted nowhere and have no rights, no money, no legal existence, no identity. To all intents and purposes, they don't exist. But, for those who look into the hidden corners they are not invisible. They may be begging on street corners, hiding away from public view, even imprisoned in sexual or domestic slavery. It is time to offer healing, to give them justice, homes and security. It is time to bring them into the light.

There are many organisations that work with asylum seekers, including survivors of trafficking, once they have come forward, had their status confirmed and been referred. But Ghost-rescue does more. It works with those who are still incarcerated, and those who don't trust statutory agencies or the police not to detain them here or to send them back to places of danger.

The steps for GRUK are:

- Identify
- Contact
- Rescue
- Make safe
- Plan future

We will, when appropriate and when it will not endanger our clients, work with partner organisations.

If you know the whereabouts of someone you believe to be trafficked, please let us know. Everything you tell us will be in the strictest confidence. If you would like to get involved, please get in touch. Anyone who works with us has to go through a strict vetting procedure, and needs to understand that rescue and the aftermath can bring considerable risk. Traffickers are usually brutal, don't let go easily, and are often backed by large and powerful organisations.

Chapter 32

As Emma sat on the train on her way in to London for the march, she couldn't believe what she was doing. This wasn't her. But then over recent months her sense of self seemed to have changed. Emma thought over her conversation with Nicola. She'd told the younger woman that she didn't understand Julian's need to get involved, but even as she'd said it, Emma had felt for the first time that she did now, this time, have some sense of why. Having seen the girl, she could no longer stay detached; it made her own concerns paltry, of little importance.

It was time she saw Posy again. Maybe she could just raise it, just vaguely, in principle, and see what she said. She felt very uncertain. She was sure that Posy was on the side of the angels, but very much didn't want to put her in an awkward position. Or put that poor girl, Veronika, in danger. As someone brought up to respect the law of the land, Emma was aware for the first time of a potential gulf between rectitude and authority. It was acutely uncomfortable.

She had arranged to meet Nicola at midday. The march was set to start off at 12.30 from Broadcasting House. According to Denise, marches increasingly left from there in the (usually vain) hope that the BBC would cover the event. They would then make their way down to Trafalgar Square for speeches, then on to the Transport for London building.

Emma very rarely came up to London at weekends – she had quite enough of the commute during the week – but this was special and for once there were no engineering works. As usual these days she had had trouble deciding what to wear. Apart from the weather (showers forecast) her own body temperature was so unreliable. In the end she wore a short mac over trousers and a few thin tops that could be put on or taken off. It had been a muggy night and she hadn't slept much. She was sweating already and trembling with nerves, but she had put the seeds in her bag, and clutched them to her like a talisman.

Nicola had suggested that they meet on the steps of All Soul's, so that they would be sure to see each other, and it was a huge relief to see the younger woman already there, waving at her, together with a couple of familiar faces from the RoadPeace services. Emma was acutely apprehensive. All these people. And it was all so unpredictable. Would there be violence? Confrontation with the police? And suppose those police included a booted and uniformed Posy? Unthinkable.

The crowds were already building, with a lot of small groups, some waving placards:

GO OSLO!

EARTH FIRST

SAY NO TO CARS

DRIVE LESS, LIVE MORE

A few banners were being unfurled: Newbury Green Party, Reclaim the Streets, Oxford Quakers, and a number of individuals handing out leaflets. There were already sounds of instruments warming up, one or two people strapping on drums. Clothes of all sorts. A top hat, a man on stilts, T-shirts. Old friends hugging. There was a surprisingly festive air.

Emma was amazed at the numbers. She saw groups she might have expected, such as the Socialist Workers and Friends of the Earth but also lots of families and groups of friends. Children, a few wheelchairs – some from her own group. A lot of flags – Norwegian, naturally, and was that German? People were enthusiastically waving other flags she didn't recognise. She turned to Nicola, who nodded.

"Yes, it is German. Did you know that they've got a completely separate cycle highway that's entirely car-free? And the one the young woman in the red bobble hat is holding is Spanish and that one over there, behind the column, is Columbian. Bogota is really at the forefront of pedestrianisation, and Hamburg and Madrid have got great plans. Even Paris has had car-free days. Everyone's at it, except us. High time we caught up!"

To her delight Emma saw Denise pushing through the crowds towards them. She'd expected her to march under a different banner – after all, RoadPeace was her concern, rather than her sister's.

As Denise hugged her, Emma expressed her surprise.

"But of course I'm coming with you. It's your first march, after all! And," as she squeezed Emma's arm, "I know how much this means to you." Emma swallowed. Yes, but how lovely that Denise understood that and was coming with her. Nicola had her own, and more recent, grief to deal with.

Emma was surprised how well organised it was. Despite all the different groups, there were barricades in the middle of the street as they walked, stewards in day-glo tabards, keeping them on track, and several policemen walking alongside, quite jolly, presumably quite used to this sort of thing. As they walked at a slowish but steady pace, Denise was, of course, chatting to other walkers. Even as she envied her sister's easy sociability, Emma sensed in herself a warmth, a feeling of pride and – could it be? – that dreaded word, "solidarity". She couldn't join in the familiar banter of Denise and the others, but felt a little less on the margins, a little less alone. Activist? No, she'd leave that to the others, but it was good to feel an inkling of what it was to be part of something bigger than her own personal concerns. Even Johnny.

The noise was considerable. Some people were shouting, aggressive, angry. When they found themselves next to a particularly vocal group, Nicola shouted to her, gesturing to a group under a Quaker banner, "Let's walk with them. They're a bit quieter!" As the two of them walked together in companionable silence, Nicola said rather shyly, "You know, I was a bit nervous about coming today."

Emma turned to her in surprise. "Really? I can't imagine it." With a little self-deprecatory laugh she added, "I thought I was the only one."

But Nicola seemed to be talking to herself. "And now I feel a certain sense not just of relief but, yes, exhilaration. I feel Phil would be proud of me at last. Stepping out of my comfort zone. Standing up for what I believe in." Emma warmed at Nicola's confidences. Having got off on the wrong foot with her, she'd been a bit daunted at the younger woman's self-assurance, and had taken a while to find her own balance.

Once they'd got away from the noisy crowd, they found that many others were walking quietly in pairs or small groups, talking to each other All in all, Emma found it surprising how good-natured it was, even jolly, with music, people jigging as they walked, some singing. She had expected something more obviously serious, in keeping with the solemnity of the subject. But apparently passionate protest didn't stop people having fun. In some ways it seemed more about comradeship than protest, but there was no doubting the commitment of people prepared to turn out for hours of exposure to the cold. When Emma expressed her surprise at seeing people from all over the country – from Salisbury, Bristol and Leeds – for what was, after all, a London concern, Denise replied, hotly: "Why wouldn't they? We all walk on the same earth."

At Trafalgar Square there was a makeshift platform, the organising of microphones, then speeches: from Jeremy Corbyn, someone from Friends of the Earth and some man whose name she didn't get, who was leader of one of the unions. The speeches were punctuated by cheers, shouted comments and the occasional boo. Emma's feet hurt. Walking slowly was tiring, and there was too much standing around. It all began to feel interminable.

Eventually they moved on, in smaller numbers now, to

Victoria and the offices of Transport for London.

"Not that we have anything against TFL," Nicola said as they walked, "it's just a symbol." She explained that the Department of Transport would have been more influential, but, as it was embedded in among other buildings, it simply wasn't suitable. "I should know," Nicola said. "It's bang opposite my office." She said that some of the activists (not her: she had to keep her head down) had thoroughly researched the TFL building and its surrounds.

As the group walked in convoy along Victoria Street, banners waving, Emma found herself on familiar territory. On bus days, this was on her daily route home. As always, she found the conglomeration of huge plate glass buildings offensively blank, only the glimpse of an occasional spire a welcome reminder of finer proportions. Amid the barricades of seemingly endless developments there was, thankfully, the occasional little old brick-built house that obstinately held its place. The scene was thoroughly familiar and, as always, Emma gave thanks that her little hamlet was too insignificant to be "developed", and was left pretty much alone.

At least on a Saturday afternoon, the drills had fallen silent and the gangly cranes, competing for height with the skyscrapers, were stationery. She'd never taken any notice of the TFL building, which was just where the bus turned into Victoria Street towards the station. It was made of a rather ugly mottled brown stone or possibly marble, probably twenty storeys high. She could see what Nicola meant: there was space to get all the way round, with gardens on one side that they might be able to sit in later. There was even a handy bike docking station for a quick getaway!

As they walked up to the building, protesters were handing out leaflets to passers-by and a cordon of police was already in place, their backs to the building to stop any attempts at entry. Their group collected on the pavement facing the building, stewards taking care to see that they didn't block the highway and, as the numbers grew, they gradually spread out round the sides. It took a long time for the tail to arrive but, eventually, through a loud hailer, a young man shouted instructions.

"We're going to circle the building. Space yourselves out, hold hands or link arms where you can."

The police were suddenly more evident, moving forward to ensure no one got too close to the building. So were the press, flashbulbs flashing. Nicola averted her head, trying to ensure she didn't get captured on film, though, what the hell, she couldn't hide forever.

Sensing Emma's anxiety, Nicola and Denise shepherded her round to the other side of the building, where it was a bit quieter. "Don't worry," Nicola whispered, "We've got permission. We're not doing anything illegal." Grasping Denise's arm, she said: "There won't be any trouble, will there, Denise?"

Denise grinned and shook her head. "Of course not."

And, then, as if by magic, the music began. A young woman had attached a loudspeaker to her phone, and gradually, in response to her broadcast calling, those on either side of Emma began to sway, until, smiling and linking hands, the whole massive chain of protesters began to move in a giant clockwise circle.

With heart fluttering and her precious bag slung close to her chest, Emma took Nicola's outstretched hand and linked with others whose lives she had yet to touch. So, holding hands, Emma looking straight ahead, Nicola looking at Emma, they slowly began to dance.

* * *

LondonNewsOnline

South London home hit a second time

The fire service was called to a Lambeth house in the early hours of Tuesday morning, but was too late to save much of the building. It is not known how the fire started, but police say that they are treating it as suspicious. There are no known casualties. The terraced building had previously been used by homeless people in the area, but it is understood that it has been empty since the death of a young charity worker on the doorstep last year. The death was originally found to be accidental; police would not say whether there were any plans to re-open the case.

Epilogue

It is just before midnight on one of the longest days of the year. A straight-backed young woman in a long flowing skirt stands on an isolated pier on a remote island off the West coast of Scotland. Her waist-length black hair is partially covered by a shawl and on the ground in front of her is a small leather case containing her new papers and all her worldly belongings. Holding her hand is an equally straight-backed little girl with eyes of different colours. The two of them are looking out to sea, waiting for deliverance.

About the author

Jennifer Kavanagh worked in publishing for nearly thirty years, the last fourteen as an independent literary agent. In the past twenty years she has run a community centre in London's East End, worked with street homeless people and refugees, and set up microcredit programmes in London, and in Africa. She has also worked as a research associate for the Prison Reform Trust.

Jennifer is a Quaker. She now spends most of her time writing, speaking, and running retreats. She has published ten books of non-fiction and two previous novels. Fiction has always been her first love.

Other novels by Jennifer Kavanagh

The Emancipation of B

B is not a child of his time. As an outsider, he hides his secrets well. Freedom is all he dreams of. But when it comes at last, it is in the most unexpected way – and at a considerable cost.

"A hymn to mindfulness and a moving meditation on our conflicting ideas of home in a novel that explores one solitary man's efforts to find sanctuary in the most unlikely of places."
Paul Wilson, author of *The Visiting Angel*

"I think the book is wonderful. Vivid and absorbing and thought-provoking. B is an odd character, yes, but I found myself really caring what became of him. Chapeau, as they say in France!"
Tony Peake, author of *A Summer Tide, Son to the Father, Seduction* and a biography of Derek Jarman

"I was completely hooked all the way through. You simply had to turn the page! The book is both haunting and memorable."
Laura Morris, literary agent

The Silence Diaries

Suzie and Orbs are in their thirties and have been together for a couple of years. Orbs reluctantly makes a living in the City and Suzie is a respected financial journalist, but each has another life hidden from the outside world...

Their secret existence is threatened first when Suzie is offered a highly visible job, and then by an accident that turns their lives upside down. This is their struggle to survive as partners.

"The quiet strength of *The Silence Diaries* is the way extraordinary people – a Fool, a political ventriloquist and a hearer of voices – are seen engaged in the everyday struggle for closeness and authenticity, a drama that resolves itself not in twists and denouements but in human virtues: patience, kindness and

mutual understanding."
Philip Gross, winner of the T.S. Eliot Prize 2009

"A sweet and gentle novel about how hard it can be to communicate honestly with others and be our real selves. In the frenzied, inauthentic world we have created, this is a book that reveals how the search for what is real and meaningful can sometimes be realised in unorthodox places: in the wisdom of fooling, the consolations of silence, not to mention the truculence of Bruce the ventriloquist's fox."
Paul Wilson, winner of the Portico prize, author of *The Visiting Angel*

ROUNDFIRE
BOOKS

FICTION

Put simply, we publish great stories. Whether it's literary or popular, a gentle tale or a pulsating thriller, the connecting theme in all Roundfire fiction titles is that once you pick them up you won't want to put them down.
If you have enjoyed this book, why not tell other readers by posting a review on your preferred book site.

Recent bestsellers from Roundfire are:

The Bookseller's Sonnets
Andi Rosenthal

The Bookseller's Sonnets intertwines three love stories with a tale of religious identity and mystery spanning five hundred years and three countries.

Paperback: 978-1-84694-342-3 ebook: 978-184694-626-4

Birds of the Nile
An Egyptian Adventure
N.E. David

Ex-diplomat Michael Blake wanted a quiet birding trip up the Nile – he wasn't expecting a revolution.

Paperback: 978-1-78279-158-4 ebook: 978-1-78279-157-7

Blood Profit$
The Lithium Conspiracy
J. Victor Tomaszek, James N. Patrick, Sr.

The blood of the many for the profits of the few… *Blood Profit$* will take you into the cigar-smoke-filled room where American policy and laws are really made.

Paperback: 978-1-78279-483-7 ebook: 978-1-78279-277-2

The Burden
A Family Saga
N.E. David

Frank will do anything to keep his mother and father apart. But he's carrying baggage – and it might just weigh him down …

Paperback: 978-1-78279-936-8 ebook: 978-1-78279-937-5

The Cause
Roderick Vincent
The second American Revolution will be a fire lit from an internal spark.
Paperback: 978-1-78279-763-0 ebook: 978-1-78279-762-3

Don't Drink and Fly
The Story of Bernice O'Hanlon: Part One
Cathie Devitt
Bernice is a witch living in Glasgow. She loses her way in her life and wanders off the beaten track looking for the garden of enlightenment.
Paperback: 978-1-78279-016-7 ebook: 978-1-78279-015-0

Gag
Melissa Unger
One rainy afternoon in a Brooklyn diner, Peter Howland punctures an egg with his fork. Repulsed, Peter pushes the plate away and never eats again.
Paperback: 978-1-78279-564-3 ebook: 978-1-78279-563-6

The Master Yeshua
The Undiscovered Gospel of Joseph
Joyce Luck
Jesus is not who you think he is. The year is 75 CE. Joseph ben Jude is frail and ailing, but he has a prophecy to fulfil …
Paperback: 978-1-78279-974-0 ebook: 978-1-78279-975-7

On the Far Side, There's a Boy
Paula Coston
Martine Haslett, a thirty-something 1980s woman, plays hard on the fringes of the London drag club scene until one night which prompts her to sign up to a charity. She writes to a young Sri Lankan boy, with consequences far and long.
Paperback: 978-1-78279-574-2 ebook: 978-1-78279-573-5

Tuareg
Alberto Vazquez-Figueroa
With over 5 million copies sold worldwide, *Tuareg* is a classic adventure story from best-selling author Alberto Vazquez-Figueroa, about honour, revenge and a clash of cultures.
Paperback: 978-1-84694-192-4

Readers of ebooks can buy or view any of these bestsellers by clicking on the live link in the title. Most titles are published in paperback and as an ebook. Paperbacks are available in traditional bookshops. Both print and ebook formats are available online.

Find more titles and sign up to our readers' newsletter at
http://www.johnhuntpublishing.com/fiction

Follow us on Facebook at https://www.facebook.com/JHPfiction
and Twitter at https://twitter.com/JHPFiction